THE LEGENDS OF GREEMULAX

KIMMY SCHMIDT
with Sarah Mlynowski

LITTLE, BROWN AND COMPANY
New York Boston

Copyright © 2019 Universal Studios.
Unbreakable Kimmy Schmidt is a trademark and copyright of Universal Television.
Licensed by Universal Studios 2019.
All Rights Reserved.

Illustrations and cover art by Brandon Dorman
Illustration on page 213 by Danh Nguyen

Little, Brown and Company
Hachette Book Group
1290 Avenue of the Americas, New York, NY 10104
Visit us at LBYR.com

First Edition: April 2019

Little, Brown and Company is a division of Hachette Book Group, Inc. The Little, Brown name and logo are trademarks of Hachette Book Group, Inc.

The publisher is not responsible for websites (or their content) that are not owned by the publisher.

Library of Congress Control Number: 2019933519

ISBNs: 978-0-316-53575-5 (hardcover), 978-0-316-53574-8 (ebook)

Printed in the United States of America

LSC-H

10 9 8 7 6 5 4 3 2 1

To boys and girls equally

THE LEGEND OF GARATE PRACTICE

Deep in the scorched woods of North Greem-ulax, where the Grabagorns ruled, Penn sat on a spiky log, watching his friends roll around and kick each other. "Good defense!" Penn said, debating if he should jump in or wait for the next match. He didn't want to interrupt, but he was itching to get in some swings.

Garate—Grabagorn karate—required at least one other guy to kick, chop, and punch, so Penn usually spent his days with his three best friends, practicing their moves. Four was the ideal number.

Today, only the twins—Landon and Brandon—had shown up. Marcus was late. They had to get started without him, since members of the Grabagorn brotherhood were required to do at least nine hours of Garate practice a day. If they didn't complete this training, they would never be strong enough to fight in any brawl, let alone survive a dragon invasion.

Ever since the Great Scorch, Grabagorns were always, *always* preparing for another dragon invasion.

Landon and Brandon were already covered in black grime from head to toe. Landon's sandy hair now looked muddy. They had begun practicing the hardest Garate move of all—the Roundpit. In order to perform this incredibly advanced move, one had to spin around ten times and then kick a dragon directly in the armpit. Grabagorn Prime told them that if performed correctly, the Roundpit would kill a dragon instantly. Just fire and blood everywhere!

"Watch this!" Brandon, the taller twin, barked at Penn and Landon. His tangled black hair and pale, skinny neck reminded Penn of a pencil. "I'll show you guys how to Roundpit like a real Grabagorn," Brandon said. He readied himself against the side of the arena and flung his lanky body into a series of spins. Penn still wasn't used to seeing Brandon with his blue, shaggy Grabagorn feet. They'd only popped out two weeks ago, but Brandon seemed to be getting better at walking on them every day. After ten rotations, Brandon sprang forward on his massive feet and kicked the charred tree stump that was playing the role of dragon. The tree shattered into smoky, black bits and sent a haze of dust into his brother's face.

Brandon cheered while Landon coughed.

"Did you see that?" Brandon asked. "I killed it! I'm amazing! That dragon was toast!"

"Yeah, nice one," Penn said, although he worried a real dragon would have been the one to turn *Brandon* to toast. But ever since his friend had started to transformate, Brandon thought he was *amazing* at everything. His ego had gotten as big as his new blue feet.

Penn knew that transformating was only the beginning. Once Brandon became a full-grown Grabagorn, he would be enormous and strong, with icy blue skin and a set of horns. That was when he would become a true man, according to Grabagorn Prime. Penn wasn't so sure. But then again, Penn was only twelve, still all boy. No big

Grabagorn feet in sight. Not even a big Grabagorn toe. Not even a big Grabagorn toenail.

The truth was, Penn wasn't sure he wanted a Grabagorn toenail. Or toe. Or foot. Or anything Grabagorn at all.

The more Grabagorny someone became, the less he laughed. Although Penn noticed that the elders did still laugh *at* him, if not with him. But they were kind of mean, and Penn didn't like being mean.

He knew he had no choice, though.

It was only a few months ago, at this year's SuperCup, that Penn noticed he and his friends were the only ones left who were still all boy.

Everyone in North Greemulax came together on the SuperCup, the most important day of the year. They strapped on their strongest gear and got in line, hiking up the snaking footpaths of Grabagorn Mountain to the chief Man Cave to retell the story of the Great

Scorch, mourn their losses, celebrate their strength, and then, finally, compete in Garate. The winner of the competition took home the SuperCup, an actual cup made of stone.

First they ate a hearty feast of meat stew. After the meal, the Grabagorns, part-Grabagorns, and boys all gathered around to listen to the tale of their greatest battle.

"Ten years ago, before the Great Scorch, our community was not only home to us, but lots and lots of womenfolk," Grabagorn Prime explained. His massive beard, covered in cheese dust and tobacco spit, shook as he spoke. "They were beautiful to look at but mouthy. With hair for smelling!"

As was customary during this part of the story, the Grabagorns threw their heads back, howling in honor of the memory of the womenfolk and the loss of something good-looking. Penn didn't remember the women.

He dreamt about what he imagined women to be, but he really had no idea. He'd been only two years old during the Great Scorch, the youngest of the community. And since all the women were gone, he was the youngest still.

"The dragons preyed on our weakness. The dragons burned our land and killed our women. Why? Because we were too *weak* to defend them!"

A guy sitting up front, Grabagoop, slammed the ground in frustration. "KILL THE DRAGONS!" This set off Grabagreen, who punched Grabagul, which quickly sent the whole crew into a round of angry stomping.

Penn looked around the cave and realized that he and his friends were the only ones who hadn't transformed at all. Everyone else had at least a little Grabagorn to them. An ear. A chin. An elbow.

"We must fight!" Grabagorn Prime hollered, getting the whole cave going again. "We must practice our Garate!" The crowd cheered. Grabagorn Prime lifted his huge blue arms and balled his paws into fists. "We will be ready for those nasty dragons . . . that is, if they ever dare to *try* to enter our land again. In the old days, society wanted us to suppress our strongness. They wanted us to wear sweaters and floss our teeth. They wanted us to take turns being in charge."

The Grabagorns all booed, as was the custom. Grabagorn Prime was yelling now.

"They made us *weak*. That's why those fire monsters were able to defeat us. It was only after the Great Scorch that we could no longer avoid our destiny. From the tragedy, our true hairy giant Grabagorn selves emerged—like the first issue of a cool comic book. Now we know that men are destined to become Grabagorns. We were weak then, but now we are strong! When I say, 'Grabagorn,' you say, 'Great chant!' Grabagorn."

"Great chant!"

"Grabagorn."

"Great chant!"

"We need to be tough!" shouted Grabagork, who just a month earlier had been a
boy called William. (Only those who had
turned all Grabagorn got to take Grabagorn
names.) "We need to be mean!" he added. As
he snarled, Penn noticed that William—no,
Grabagork—began to sprout an extra tuft of fur
on his back. It seemed like the more noise the
guy made, the Grabagornier he got. Grabagork stood up and pounded his chest. "For
the women! For the women!" he chanted, and
soon everyone had joined in.

"We need more traps," Grabagoop said.

Penn perked up. He may have been the youngest, but he was good at making traps. He had just
made one with pulleys and big round rocks that
rolled down a slope and triggered a lever when
it caught something. That was another reason

he wasn't looking forward to transformating—he could see that the elders couldn't make small things with their big hands. Grabagorn hands only made good fists. Their hands couldn't make tight knots for strong traps. That's why his traps were so good. He hadn't caught a dragon, though. Nobody had ever caught one. Not yet.

Back in the practice arena, Penn heard Landon shout, "Penn! Come rumble with me!" "I want to Garate-chop you with my new Grabagorn paw." Landon held up his left hand, which had just this week turned the signature blue color and begun to sprout tufts of coarse, blue hair. Landon smiled proudly at his achievement, and Penn noticed that the tips of his friend's teeth had begun to sharpen as well. Now everyone had started to transformate.

Brandon.

Landon.

Even Marcus.

Everyone but Penn.

Out of place again.

If he really thought about it, maybe Penn had always felt out of place.

"Be right there," Penn called back, even as his whole body filled with nerves at the thought of when he might start to transformate. He glanced down at his own small hand and wiggled his fingers, trying to imagine them with blue hair growing out of the knuckles. Penn quite liked how they looked now. Maybe there was a way to avoid it....Hadn't Grabagorn Prime himself said that back before the Great Scorch, the men didn't always transformate all the way into Grabagorns? Penn's mind began to wander, but he quickly pushed the thoughts away and hopped down into the pit. He used to be able to talk about this kind of stuff with Marcus, but if the twins found out about his hesitation, they'd tease him endlessly. All boys wanted to become big, tough Grabagorns! He put up his fists and took a defensive Garate stance. He still had nearly eight hours of practice to complete today.

"I'll take you down, Landon," Penn growled, trying to sound tough. "You're such a Weaklink. You're never gonna be a full Grabagorn." Penn had seen other boys say this to each other, and it always made them really mad.

It worked.

Landon's face twisted into a dreadful scowl, and he growled and roared and wumped as he charged, taking Penn down.

Landon and Brandon may have been strong, but Penn was nimble. And he was fast.

"Grrrraagghh!" Landon gurgled, raising his paw high above his head. In a swift motion, he slammed it down, aiming for Penn's shoulder. But Penn was too quick, rolling out of harm's way. Poor Landon swung his paw down with such intensity that it cracked the hard ground and was now lodged in the dried mud. Penn tried not to laugh, but Landon looked so goofy struggling and squirming to release it. Penn couldn't help it. He giggle-snorted.

"Where is Marcus, anyway?" Brandon wondered aloud as he reached for Landon, pulling his brother back to his feet. "Pretty lame of him to ditch practice."

"I don't know." Penn helped himself up and tried to brush the dirt off his clothes. It made no difference anyway. Everything the Grabagorns wore was either brown or black, though none of it had started out that color.

He hopped up to the ridge and scanned the horizon. It was the same old view—a million blackened tree trunks and Grabagorn Mountain in the distance.

As it often did, Penn's mind jumped to the worst-case scenario: Marcus had been eaten by

13

a dragon. After all, it had been over an hour since they were supposed to meet, and there was still no sign of their friend. Marcus was his best and most reliable friend, although things had changed between them since Marcus had started to transformate. They used to tell stories to each other about their mothers, even though neither of them had real memories to rely on. But Marcus no longer wanted to talk about his mom. "Do you think... something happened to him?"

"Not sure," Brandon said, taking a gigantic swig of well water from his bottle.

Penn did the same. The liquid tasted even sweeter after an intense Garate fight. Too sweet, as usual. But he forced some down.

"If he did get eaten by a dragon..." Brandon mused, pausing for dramatic effect, "I call dibs on his Man Cave. I'm gonna need my own space now that I'm becoming a Graba-gorn. Can't be sharing with my stupid twin."

"You can have his if I get ours," Landon said. "Ours is better."

While the twins argued over who would hypothetically get dibs and who was, in fact, stupid, Penn tried to push away the image of Marcus sitting inside the belly of an evil dragon.

After another couple of practice rounds, the boys were hitting their stride.

"Youf gufs!" A strange voice echoed through the dead trees. Penn, Brandon, and Landon spun around and sprang to their feet, ready to attack. Penn was relieved to see it was Marcus, running up the hill and practically tripping over his own feet with sheer excitement. "PFENN! Your traf cauf somfing! Iff inth the thrap!" Drool dribbled down his chin, and his blue tongue lolled out of his mouth.

"What?!" Penn replied, having no clue what his friend was saying. The one part of Marcus that had started to transformate into Grabagorn was his mouth, which had made talking a challenge for him.

Marcus put his hands on his knees, catching his breath. He wiped the back of his hand against his slobbery blue lips and tried again. This time, he spoke slower.

"Penn, your trap caught something!" Marcus said. "Well, *three* somethings."

"My trap caught three dragons?!" Penn felt like his chest was going to burst open. He'd never even seen one dragon. And now there were three. In *his* trap. Grabagorn Prime was going to lose his mind. Penn almost hugged

Landon and Brandon but then thought better of it. Grabagorns didn't hug.

Penn grabbed his rucksack and bottle. "I want to see the dragons!"

"Yeah..." Marcus said, a funny expression on his face. "I'm not actually sure *what* they are. You better come look."

Not dragons? What else could they be?

THE LEGEND OF THE DRAGON TRAP

Penn's heart pounded violently as he and the other boys followed Marcus through the wilds of North Greemulax. "Hurry!" Penn yelled as he leaped over a charred tree stump. "Can't you guys move any faster?"

"I can," Brandon bragged, then ran ahead on his big Grabagorn feet.

As he sped across the charred pitlands, through the abandoned Radio Shack, and past the Man Caves, Penn secretly worried that whatever he had caught would find a way out of his trap before he could see them. Even though this particular trap was his best creation yet (according to a few of the toughest Grabagorns who had tested it), Penn suddenly felt less confident about his design. It had been devised with dragons in mind. And there were so many weird variables that had to be accounted for, like fire breath and wingspan. Who knew what magical powers his new mystery catch might have?

When they arrived at the streambed, it meant that they were almost there. Marcus led the way, hopping onto the splintered-log bridge and running across quickly. It was definitely going to crumble and snap soon, so no one tempted fate by spending more time on it than they had to. But most of the stuff in North

Greemulax was falling apart, probably because ever since Grabanap took over as chief repair officer, the Repair Force seemed to spend their time playing Grabagolf and arm wrestling instead of fixing things.

"Ofverf fere!" Marcus yelled as the boys finally crested the hill, accidentally spraying them with droplets of slobber. The trap still had the three creatures inside!

Marcus darted behind a giant boulder and motioned for the others to join him. Penn was dying to get a closer look. From this distance, it was impossible to tell what these creatures were.

"Fudge! How did this happen to us?" shouted one of the creatures. Then a small hand poked through the net! It had five slim fingers and no fur, just like Penn's hand. "Are you sure you can't get us out of here, X?" Its voice was high and squeaky, but pleasant. It sounded familiar and warm. Like sunshine.

At this, Landon perked up. "Did you hear that? They're speaking our language."

The boys peeked out from behind the boulder, moving a little closer but careful to stay hidden. Brandon sniffed the air. "And they don't smell like farts and beard mold."

Landon used his Grabagorn paw to punch his brother in the arm. "Are those . . . *womenfolk*?"

Penn's heart skipped a beat.

"What are you talking about?" Brandon rubbed his freshly punched arm. "Womenfolk don't exist anymore. They were killed by the dragons. Everyone knows that."

"But I remember them from when we were kids," Landon said. "And they looked just like *that*." He pointed to the trap, where three distinct outlines now stood, calm. "Like us. But a little different."

It was much easier to make out the shape of them when they were closer. They did look like humans. . . . But how was that possible? Penn's mixture of excitement and fear at the prospect of seeing dragons turned into complete confusion. Yeah, he wanted to see a dragon. But he'd also spent his whole life wondering about women—what they looked like, sounded like, how long their beards were, if his dreams about them were anything even close to reality—and now here they were?

Penn couldn't wait any longer. He had to get a closer look to confirm Landon's theory. Penn crouched down and moved slowly so as not to attract the attention of the creatures. After all, it would be foolish for the boys to reveal themselves before they knew exactly what they were dealing with.

But Penn couldn't tear his eyes away from the trap, so he didn't notice the stinkhole until it was too late. "Arrrgyle!" he called out in pain, sounding uncharacteristically Grabagorny as his left foot broke through the soft spot in the ground. It released a pocket of purple, smelly gas.

Immediately, the creatures spun around and faced Penn, their big eyes blinking at him through the netting as they started to cough from the disgusting stench. For a brief moment, they all stood frozen, staring at one another in shocked surprise.

"Hey! You over there!" the smallest one yelled to Penn. Her voice didn't sound like sunshine anymore. It was loud and scary. "Help us! We're trapped!"

But the boys didn't help. They panicked. And ran.

"Wait!" the smallest one called out again, voice full of desperation. "Don't go!"

Penn was surprised by the sympathetic tug he felt at his heart, and he stopped short. But then his Grabagorn instinct kicked in. The creatures didn't look menacing, but who knew what they were capable of? There was no way he was about to unleash them into North Greemulax to wreak havoc on the brotherhood! No, the *right* thing was to tell the elders about it. Grabagorn Prime would know what to do.

Penn clambered down the hill. He didn't even look back over his shoulder at the creatures, just in case seeing their sad eyes would make him change his mind.

The boys ran to the caves at double speed, straight to the mess cavern, interrupting what looked like a very important meeting of the Grabagorn elders.

A chorus of angry snorts, followed by the raising of fists, signaled that an intense competition was currently underway. Grabagorn Prime and Grabalook sat across a table from each other, making the meanest expressions they could muster. The rest of the elders stood around them in a circle, cheering. At the sound of a Grabagornian horn, they squared their shoulder and gripped each other's hand, elbows on the table.

The horn sounded once more, and the arm wrestling began. Grabagorns applauded as the two struggled to keep their forearms up, grunting with each action. Grabagorn Prime's glasses were getting fogged up. And his arm was dangerously close to the table.

Landon leaned into Penn and whispered, "This doesn't seem like a good time to—"

"Weaklinks!" Grabagorn Prime bellowed. "I was just about to stop letting him think he was going to win!" He jumped up, a loud thump sounding as his opponent's hand crashed onto the table, and he stomped over to the boys.

Grabagorn Prime smiled, then stiffened.

"The boys need me. It's urgent," he called out. "I was obviously about to win, but now I must go."

Wow, Penn thought, they hadn't even said anything and Grabagorn Prime knew what they had to tell him was important. He was such a great leader.

Grabagorn Prime wiped sweat from his hairy brow and ushered the boys out of the cavern. "Okay, what's up, Weaklinks?"

Penn cleared his throat and went for it. "My trap caught something. Actually, *three* somethings."

"Dragons?!" Grabagorn Prime replied with surprise.

"Well..." Penn looked up at him. "Not exactly."

"C'mon, boys, spit it out." He was starting to look mad.

Penn glanced at his friends to see if any

of them might want to explain. They were all looking at the ground.

Penn took a deep breath. "We think they might be . . . *womenfolk*."

Grabagorn Prime's expression changed about ten times before landing on skeptical. "Show me," he said.

The entire way back to the trap, Grabagorn Prime kept insisting that the creatures were probably just large birds. He knew for a fact that every single woman had perished in the Great Scorch.

"Every. Single. One," he said. "All of them. Gone."

Penn didn't want to argue with him, because he was in charge, after all. And he was enormous. But Penn knew that Grabagorn

Prime was in for a shock. Large birds did not speak their language.

By the time they arrived back at the trap, the sun was beginning to set over North Greemulax. It was the prettiest time—the golden hour. On a normal day, Penn would have been sitting with his friends, sharing a cup of grape juice as they watched the charred landscape turn from golden gray to golden dark gray to black. But today was anything but normal.

"Hey, you came back!" shouted one of the creatures. It had red hair.

"Let us out!" another demanded, poking its angry fists through the net. Penn began to feel incredibly guilty. This was not what the trap had been intended for.

But Grabagorn Prime didn't let them out.

Instead, the big, blue leader pulled the boys aside. His face was alight with an excitement that Penn had never seen before. Grabagorn

Prime almost looked...*happy*? "Boys, you did the right thing by coming to me first." He stroked his wiry beard and narrowed his eyes. "But you were wrong. These aren't large birds. . . . These are women."

"That's what we—" Penn started.

"You were wrong," he repeated.

Penn couldn't wrap his mind around what was happening, even though he'd known in his bones the moment he laid eyes on them that those really were women. But how was it possible? "Didn't the dragons kill all the women?"

"It seems that a few of them escaped the Great Scorch," Grabagorn Prime explained, as if he was telling them something as simple as what was on the menu for Later Day Meal. "It's a miracle they have survived for this long without the protection of us Grabagorns! They are so fragile and weak."

The angry words coming from the trap suggested otherwise.

"We can hear you!"

"Rude!"

"We're not weak."

Grabagorn Prime brought the four boys into a huddle—the most sacred of bonds. "We will keep the women safe! Because that is our job as Grabagorns."

Penn and his friends all nodded their heads in agreement, since it seemed like Grabagorn Prime was looking for some kind of response from them.

"Alright, then." Grabagorn Prime broke the huddle and put his massive paws on his hips. "Now let's move these womenfolk somewhere special."

"Let us out!" one of the taller women shouted from the bottom of the ten-foot pit they'd been moved to. "Enough is enough already!" She had long, brown hair. Penn had never seen anything so shiny. Except maybe the women's outfits, which were glittery and made out of more colors than he previously believed to exist.

"You can't just throw us in a pit against our will," the other tall one said. "There are rules!"

"Oh, but I can!" Grabagorn Prime said. "And I did."

Brandon laughed.

"Calm down, girls." Grabagorn Prime used his most soothing voice as he kneeled at the edge and talked down to the women. "We know you're scared. Don't worry. We are Grabagorns and we are going to protect you. But you have to be good."

"Just let us go!" the other tall one growled. She had glowing yellow hair. "We have places to be, you know."

Grabagorn Prime belly-laughed. "I forgot how charming womenfolk are when they get upset. It is very cute!" He shook his head with a smile and began to pace back and forth. "You ladies will be very comfortable in the pit."

The dark-haired one yelled, "You monsters!"

Penn couldn't help looking their way, and as he did, he locked eyes with the smallest one, the one with red hair. That tiny, nagging feeling telling Penn that something wasn't right was still there. And that word: *monster*. Is that what they were? They did fight all day and live in a desolate wasteland. . . .

Penn took a couple steps back, preferring that the women think he had nothing to do with the whole operation. That is, if women could

have thoughts that complex. The way Grabagorns talked about womenfolk made it seem like
they were pretty to look at but kind of dumb.

"Don't worry, boys," Grabagorn Prime
said as he pressed the button to activate the
five men who carried the glass lid for the pit.
"These women will be so much happier now
that we're keeping them safe from the wilds of
Greemulax! Trust me."

"But what about the fire monsters?" Penn
asked. "Can't dragons breathe right through
the glass?" He had a vision of glass melting
and the women being anything but safe.

Grabagorn Prime held up his index finger
like he was going to say something important.
Then he burped. And kept burping.

"Agh, a new record! Everyone applaud that
great burp."

The men rushed to seal the lid in place so
they could clap enthusiastically. The twins

laughed. Marcus had the hiccups. Penn had always trusted Grabagorn Prime—he was their leader. He was a good leader. But a seed of doubt had been planted. And then Penn realized that while Grabagorn Prime had looked happy to see the women, he hadn't looked all that surprised.

3

THE LEGEND OF THE GLASS CEILING

Kristy stretched her arms above her head and jumped. "I can't reach it! It's too high!" Her red hair bounced around her shoulders as she tried again to reach the glass ceiling of the pit. This time she got a few inches higher, but it made no difference. This was a very deep pit.

"Maybe I should take a running start?"

But Kristy had to face facts. She was too short. She was only eleven and a half—the youngest Rainbow Knight ever. It was pretty silly to think she might be able to reach the top when Exthippiane Porheep and Jackelion, who were much taller and older than her, had already tried and failed. But Kristy believed she could achieve anything if she tried hard enough! She'd learned that in the Rainbow Knight handbook. She'd also learned about glitter-making, puzzle-solving, and—most importantly—protecting the vulnerable. She'd read the book cover to cover four times just last week. The illustrations were the best. And she was a big fan of the table of contents.

Unfortunately, there was nothing in the book about escaping from Grabagornian pits.

"We're doomed," Exthippiane, whom they all called "X," said with a sigh. X picked at a patch of dried mud on her rainbow skirt, which was part of the Rainbow Knight uniform. They also wore tall silver boots and leggings, and polished metal armor. (Kristy occasionally accessorized hers with a colorful cardigan, too.) But something was off with X's face and hands. Ever since they'd gotten trapped, she seemed to be . . . fading.

Jackelion wasn't looking very well, either. The tall blond was usually the epitome of poise and confidence, even in the worst situations. But being trapped in a deep pit with a glass ceiling with only one small square for air was wreaking havoc on her skin and her attitude.

"Why did the trolley have to malfunction *right* over Grabagorn territory?" Jackelion asked. "I mean, *really*. Of all places. Now we have to escape North Greemulax all over again."

Kristy had never been to North Greemulax. Well, she had been born there, but she was just a baby when they left, so she didn't remember a thing about it. She was sort of reeling at the fact that they'd just been captured by actual Grabagorns, but there was no time to think about that.

"I've been telling you for months that Trolley 4 is the worst Rainbow Knight patrol trolley in the fleet," said X, rolling her eyes. "We should have gotten it fixed—or replaced—a long time ago."

Jackelion frowned. "X, *you* were the one who was supposed to—"

"Ladies!" Kristy interrupted. "What are Rainbow Knights famous for?"

Jackelion and X exchanged a look and shrugged.

"Helping people in need?" offered X.

"Silver armor and rainbow skirts?" Jackelion tried.

"Yes. But Rainbow Knights are also always thinking *outside the box*! Or in this case, *outside the pit*. Hah! Get it?"

Jackelion shook her head. "We can't just *think* ourselves outside this pit, Kristy, you poor little dear."

"And all of our tools are still in the trolley," X added.

"No, no, just listen: All we need to do," Kristy continued, "is get someone on the *outside* to understand our situation. Then they'll help us."

"Who would do such a thing?" Jackelion laughed. "Those boys? They were already turning into Grabagorns. You know that once the process begins, it's very hard to make them see sense."

X, who was kind of moody (she even

covered all the yellow in her Rainbow Knight uniform black because yellow was "just too bright" for her), kicked at the ground and mumbled, "It's definitely too late. Those boys have already been lost to the monster inside them. They won't help us."

Even though Kristy had only been a Rainbow Knight for a year, and even though she knew that she should listen to her wisers, she also knew that these particular wisers didn't always see the bigger picture. What if they were wrong about the boys? And Kristy had complete faith in her plan.

There *was* something she had learned from the Rainbow Knight handbook that could help: the Power of One. According to the Power of One, if you helped one person be good, you might have an impact on the people around that person, too. One person could change the world. And they only needed one person to change their world right then. "Just trust me," she insisted.

Kristy wasn't sure why, but she *knew* it would work. She had seen something in the eyes of the little one that gave her hope. "What do we have to lose? Nothing!" Kristy stomped her silver boot for emphasis.

X and Jackelion couldn't argue with that.

About an hour later, as Kristy was passing the time by counting tree branches even though X and Jackelion had asked her to please stop, they heard footsteps.

Four shadowy outlines peeked over the edge.

"Hey, guys!" Kristy popped to her feet. She gave them her friendliest smile to let them know that she was a very nice person and meant no harm. "What's up? Whatcha doin'?"

They just stared at her.

"Did a dragon get your tongue?" Kristy joked. But that was clearly the wrong thing to say, because the boys took off, again, leaving the women alone, again.

Jackelion waved goodbye to their shadows. X shrugged.

"Hot fudge!" Kristy cursed. She kicked a rock in defeat and plopped down on the ground. What were they going to do now? "If they won't even listen to me, then we truly are doomed." It was rare for Kristy to give up easily, and it didn't feel good at all. Giving up was not her jam. Her jams were grape and strawberry, end of sentence. You heard me, apricot, she thought. "I was sure that would work. I was thinking outside the pit."

"Yeah, no," X said. "We knew it wouldn't work. The women left North Greemulax for a reason."

Suddenly, one of the boys reappeared. "What did you just say?" he squeaked. His eyes were wide with interest.

He was still there. The one whose eyes had given her hope. Woot! Kristy sprang back to her feet. "About thinking outside the pit?" she asked.

"Um, no...the thing about the women leaving?" the boy replied, a little louder.

Yes, yes, yes! They had hooked him! Kristy winked at the other knights and then slowly looked up at the boy. She was careful not to make any sudden moves, since he seemed quite nervous. She had been told that men sometimes get mad when they're scared.

"Do you want to hear about the Grape

Escape?" she asked. "Why don't you help us out of here and I'll tell you all about it."

"The Great Escape? Is that like the Great Scorch?"

"No, the *Grape* Escape!" Kristy said. "Wait, what's the Great Scorch?"

They regarded each other, Kristy from the bottom of the pit, Penn from the pit's edge. Her neck was starting to cramp.

The boy bit his lip. He was clearly confused. And conflicted.

Who knew what those big Grabagorns would do to him if he got caught helping them? Or even talking to them? Kristy couldn't think about that now. She needed his help.

"What's your name?" she asked. "I'm Kristy."

He hesitated. "I'm Penn. And I . . . just don't understand how you're even here. Women can't survive without Grabagorns to protect them!"

Kristy could feel X's eyes roll.

"Listen, kid," Jackelion started, but Kristy motioned for her to shush.

"Penn, why don't you tell us what the Great Scorch is, and we'll tell you about the Grape Escape. That seems fair, right?"

Penn nodded. He told them about the dragon invasion, and Kristy used her shush hand quite a lot because X and Jackelion were having a hard time keeping it together when they heard the lies the boy had been told. He finished by describing the Great Scorch, when the dragons scorched North Greemulax, killing all the women.

"Now come closer and let me tell you about the Grape Escape," Kristy said. Penn lay down on the glass and put his ear near the square hole that had been cut for airflow. This looked incredibly silly from below, with his body smooshed up against the glass, but Kristy didn't mention it.

"Okay, so you know how you were told that all the women died in the Great Scorch?" Kristy began. "Well, we didn't. Not all of us. Obviously! Because we're here!"

As the youngest in her community, Kristy never got to tell this story to someone who hadn't heard it before. This was her big chance. "See, Penn, the first thing you should know is that the dragons didn't attack North Greemulax. They were trapped in North Greemulax."

"Just like us," X chimed in, raising a sarcastic eyebrow.

"Yes," Kristy said. "Just like us. Back then, Grabagorn Prime was in charge of the women and the men. And he did all sorts of mean stuff besides trapping dragons. He encouraged all the boys to become tough and bossy and nasty—and the more they did . . . guess what happened?"

Penn was enthralled. "What?" he replied, teetering on the edge of the glass.

"The more the men started turning into Grabagorns. And the women began to disappear!"

He blinked.

"Disappear!" she repeated, throwing her arms up in the air for emphasis. This part of the story usually got a big reaction.

Still nothing.

"Anyway, the women begged the men to free the dragons, but the men wouldn't listen. So when more dragons came to rescue their friends, which, duh, was inevitable, they scorched everything in North Greemulax." Kristy motioned to the ash and mud surrounding her as proof. "See?"

"And all the women died?" Penn asked.

"Some of them did, yes. And some of the men, too," Kristy said, hanging her head. "But it wasn't until soon after, when the men all started to transformate into full Grabagorns, that Lorianna the Wobbly decided she had had it—she was sick of watching the men work out all the time. She was tired of disappearing and having to pretend like it wasn't a big deal. So she led the rest of the women away from North Greemulax forever. If we women wanted to survive, we had to do it on our own."

"But how? How could anyone get past Grabagorn Prime?"

Jackelion laughed. Kristy shush-handed her.

"Ahhh, and that brings me to the Grape Escape," Kristy said. "The best part! The women secretly put crushed bumbleroot in the men's grape juice. Which, for the record, is not a nice thing to do. But desperate times called for desperate measures. Then they waited. When the men started to get tired, the women stole away . . ."

"Never to be seen again," Kristy, Jackelion, and X said in unison.

"I was just a baby back then, so I don't remember much," Kristy said. "But I was told that Grabagorn Prime and a few of his lackeys chased us for as long as they could . . ." She trailed off. She didn't like this part of the story because it ended with mothers and sons and sisters and brothers being separated. So she jumped ahead. "As soon as we made a new home away from the Grabagorns, women started to become like our old selves—powerful, bright, and solid. And now we live without Grabagorns. In West Greemulax. With Lorianna the Wobbly as our queen. She's cool, fun, and strong, like an elephant wearing sunglasses!"

It only took a moment for the realization to hit poor Penn—that he'd been lied to for his entire life. He got up and stalked back and forth across the glass ceiling.

"They lied to me? They lied to all of us? They didn't want us to know that you had chosen to leave, so they told us you died?! I'm so . . . so . . . ANGRY!" Penn growled.

"Penn!" Kristy gasped. "Your hand!" The boy's fist had grown to three times its normal size. It was blue. And it was hairy. It looked disgusting.

"Ahhhhh!" Penn screamed, staring at his foreign fingers. "Make it stop! I don't want to be a Grabagorn! I'm not a monster!" He ran around the edge of the pit, wailing.

"Kid!" Jackelion yelled. "Can you stop,

please? You're literally stomping on our heads."

"Well, not literally," X said. "That would hurt."

"No!" Penn cried. "I'm mad!"

Jackelion sighed. "Would you stop if I told you that there's a way to reverse the process?"

Penn stopped freaking out for a moment, clearly intrigued. Kristy was intrigued, too. This was news to her. "All you have to do is eat a Lemon Bubble. At least that's what the legends say." Jackelion shrugged. "And *Candy Every-Other-Monthly*."

"I've never heard of a Lemon Bubble."

"That doesn't mean it doesn't exist," X noted. "Until an hour ago, you thought all women were dead, yet here we are. So maybe, like, check your assumptions."

"That's an excellent point, X," Kristy said.

Penn kneeled down again and spoke straight

into the hole. "If I help you escape, will you help me find one?"

"It would be our pleasure." Kristy smiled. She'd done it. How was that for thinking outside the pit?

THE LEGEND OF TEN SECONDS

It had taken five full-grown Grabagorns to secure the heavy glass ceiling over the top of the pit. Penn stood no chance of getting the thing to budge on his own. As he stared down at the women, Penn's brain felt fuzzy. He'd spent a lot of time thinking about how to trap creatures, but he'd never had to help any escape. Plus, he couldn't stop thinking about his new Grabagorn hand, which pulsed with a strange sensation. It was all a bit much.

"Use the rope, dummy!" X called out.

"Be patient, X," he heard Kristy say. "He's a boy. He might not know things."

X sighed. "Sorry, didn't mean to be rude. But the rope they used to lower us down is probably right there. Duh."

"Oh, good idea," Penn replied, still offended that X had called him a dummy. Grabagorn Prime had said that women were always supposed to be nice. Penn shook his head. The lies just kept piling up.

He scanned the surrounding area. Sometimes, Grabagorns would hide things in the hollows of tree trunks for later. Rope and knives, mostly, but sometimes a secret snack or two. He spotted a supplies tree and jogged over. He had to move quickly. This rescue was already taking too long.

Penn reached inside the ashy trunk and felt around. He pushed aside an old pair of shoes and felt the rope. He grasped it and pulled. A packet of meat jerky fell out with it. He secured the rope around the trunk of the tree and darted back over to them.

"Grab on," he said into the hole and unfurled the rope down into the pit. Kristy, Jackelion, and X sprang to their feet and began to jump, but the rope was too short. Hmm. Maybe he could tie old shoelaces together to form a longer rope? Or he could hold on to it and—

"I got it!" Kristy said. "We'll boost each other up."

"You're the smallest," X said. "We'll lift you first."

Penn watched in awe as Jackelion and X

worked together to lift Kristy up onto their shoulders. He'd never seen such amazing teamwork. He'd never seen anything like this. Everything Penn and his friends had been taught was about fighting. If the women worked together as a team, how could they tell which of them was winning? They moved like one big creature, with Jackelion and X on the bottom and Kristy up top. Kristy raised her arms and caught the rope, shimmying her body up to meet the glass.

"I got it!" Kristy poked her head through the hole. She tried to climb higher but kept getting stuck. She twisted her shoulders and squirmed around, but she still wouldn't fit. She couldn't even get her arms out.

Kristy lost her grip, and the women tumbled to the ground. They sprang back up again, this time lifting Jackelion up.

"ROY G. BIV!" Jackelion cried as she thrust her armored elbow against the glass at full force. It was a battle cry of the Rainbow Knights. The moment the shiny metal made contact with the ceiling, a network of cracks appeared and quickly spread to its edges. One more hit, and a hunk loosened and fell to the ground. She'd done it! Jackelion had broken the glass ceiling! The others cheered as she climbed all the way up and out.

WEE-OO! WEE-OO! WEE-OO! Oh no...

An alarm?

Sirens blared as red lights flashed across the landscape.

An alarm! Penn knew they didn't have much time. It would be five minutes, max, before Grabagorn Prime showed up with a band of angry Grabagorns.

"We have to hurry!" Penn shouted as he and Jackelion pulled Kristy and X up.

"Follow me!" Jackelion said. X and Kristy obeyed and ran after her, but Penn hesitated.

Grabagorn Prime was going to be mad. Really mad. Penn imagined his mad face, eyes red and bulging. What had he done?

"Come on, Penn!" Kristy yelled. "Don't you want to find the Lemon Bubble?"

Right. He did want to find the Lemon Bubble.

He started running...and spotted Brandon, Landon, and Marcus frozen in place on the other side of the pit. Dagnabbit! Had they seen everything?

"He helpthed them escape! Pfenn'ths a traitor!" Marcus shouted. Brandon and Landon stood behind him, arms crossed. All three looked at Penn with shock and disgust. Should he turn around and convince them he'd been bewitched by the womenfolk? No. This was his one chance of stopping his Grabagorn transformation. He had to find that Lemon Bubble, and he had to find it before it was too late. His hand had already started changing—who knew if the Lemon Bubble would work on someone who had already completely transformated?

Penn could hear the wheeze of Grabagorn Prime's fleet of Grabagolf carts in the distance. It was now or never.

"Wait!" he yelled after the women. He leaped over a pile of rocks and scurried across the terrain toward them.

Free from the pit, the women were quick, darting past trees and over burnt logs. They led Penn through the woods and to the spot where they'd been caught by his trap.

The Grabagorns were not far behind.

"Our trolley...is still nearby," Kristy explained through shallow breaths. "Only our voices...can activate it...so there's no way those Grabagorns...could have moved it."

"We crashed it into a tree," Jackelion reminded her. "Just after we passed that other tree." Her eyes lit up as she pointed past Penn's shoulder. "Right there!"

"Hurry!" X hollered. Everyone ran to where the ten-foot by five-foot rainbow trolley car sat perched between two blackened trunks. It was a little dented but in pretty good shape considering.

The women scrambled up the trunk, grabbing onto the spiky branches and helping one another as they went. They were quick to reach the top, but Penn kept slipping. He was used to kicking trees, not climbing them.

"Penn, you gotta move faster!" Kristy called. She was almost to the top. Jackelion and X were already inside the trolley. He was still halfway down.

"Hello, Trolley," Jackelion said. At the sound of her voice, the trolley began to hum and whir to life. Even from halfway up the tree, Penn could see a row of multicolored lights blink on, sending rays of color across the nearby trees. What if the Grabagorns could see them, too?

"Trolley, take us to Pepperton Boulevard," she continued.

"Okay," the trolley chirped in response. "Setting course for Pepto Bismol."

The women groaned.

"Trolley 4 is the worst," Kristy said. "Come on, Penn. We gotta move." She was at the door of the trolley now.

"Kid, are you coming or what?" X said, popping her head out a window. "It's taking off."

Kristy reached down to him, but he was too far. "You can do it," she said. "Try harder."

"I *am* trying hard," Penn grunted.

"Then try faster," Kristy said. She looked into the distance. "The Grabagorns are almost here! I can see them!" She scrunched her nose. "And smell them."

"Ahhh!" Penn cried as he slid farther down

the tree. Chunks of crispy bark rained to the ground with each jab of his shoe into the trunk. When he finally stopped, Penn swung his right foot up, reaching for the broken nub of a branch. But he still couldn't get traction.

Penn remembered his new Grabagorn hand. It seemed pretty strong, so he tried gripping the branch above him, lifting his entire body up, and then repeating the process. It was working. In only a few seconds he found himself at the top, right below the trolley. But then Penn felt a tug on his foot. His first thought was that it was one of the Grabagorns pulling him down.

"Hot fudge!" Kristy exclaimed, peering down. "Your shoelace is caught. If I climb down, I can unhook it."

"There's no time," Jackelion told them. "The autofly is on and the override is broken." She gestured to the steering wheel, which was moving on its own. The trolley was beginning to float upward. "We're going right now!"

"We can't just leave Penn here," Kristy pleaded. "What about the Power of One?"

"He's not one of us. Time's up, Kristy," Jackelion said. "We have to leave without him."

Penn figured he was done for. The Grabagorn fight code dictated that if you were ever able to save yourself by sacrificing another, you should. Only the strong survive. Penn wasn't the strong.

But Kristy looked determined. She jumped out of the trolley like a cat, landing nimbly on a branch below Penn. She quickly started untangling the shoelace from the branches. As soon as he was freed, Penn and Kristy began to climb back up. But it was too late. The trolley was already taking off.

"Trolley!" X yelled as the trolley went higher and higher. "Wait for Kristy!"

"Okay," Trolley answered. "Here is a recipe for crispy cookies. One egg, two cups unbleached flour..."

The trolley rose higher and higher and swooped away like a colorful bird. It was one of the weirdest sights Penn had ever seen, and he would definitely draw a cool picture of it for his Vehicle Studies class if he ever went home. Was it magic? But there was no time to think about that now. They'd missed their chance to escape North Greemulax. And he was going to be in huge trouble with Grabagorn Prime.

Kristy jumped to the ground. "Over there," she whispered, yanking him into a thorny bush. "Don't make a peep."

Even though hundreds of spikes were poking into him and he wanted to cry, and his mind was still trying to make sense of Kristy's actions, of a *girl* protecting *him*, Penn trusted Kristy and stayed quiet. The two sat huddled together, twisted into a weird ball of limbs so that they could fit inside the prickly underbelly of the bush.

"The Weaklinks have told the truth. The womenfolk have been released," Grabagorn Prime growled. "Young Penn will pay for this when we find him. I haven't seen such treachery since the women escaped, I mean, uh, were all killed. . . . Whatever, I'm mad at Penn!"

The Grabagorns grunted in agreement and stomped their monster feet on the ground, kicking up a cloud of dust.

"But you lied!" The words escaped Penn's lips involuntarily.

Kristy's hand shot to Penn's mouth to cover it.

Grabagorn Prime turned in a circle as he looked around for what had made the noise. "Was that you, Grabaleg?"

"I didn't say anything, I swear!" Grabaleg insisted. He pointed at another Grabagorn.

"It was probably him." The Grabagorns proceeded to get into a lengthy, noisy argument about who called whom a liar.

"I know it's hard," Kristy whispered to Penn. Her voice was soft and gentle, like a rabbit right before it was prepared for Night Meal. "But we have to stay quiet. Just count to ten. You can endure anything for ten seconds. Then you'll be okay. Okay?"

Penn nodded. By the time he had counted to ten in his mind, the Grabagorns were leaving. Kristy was so smart.

"See?" Kristy smiled, eyes sparkling. "They think we were on the trolley with Jackelion and X. They won't be looking for us. We'll just have to make our own way out of North Greemulax on foot. It will be an adventure!" Kristy crawled out of the bush, her red hair all tangled and covered with burrs. But because of her metal armor, her skin was unscratched.

Penn wondered where he could get armor like that. He was going to need it.

The sun bloomed orange and pink as it peeked over the horizon and climbed up into the sky. Penn tried not to look down at the steaming crater below the rickety wire bridge. With each step, the cables felt more precarious. He worried they would snap at any second. Steam licked the bottom of his shoes and the ends of the good-for-nothing shoelaces that had gotten him and Kristy into this mess.

"West Greemulax isn't far, Penn," Kristy said. She didn't seem too bothered by the danger. She didn't seem too bothered by anything. Penn found this odd, but also . . . refreshing?

They'd been walking through North Greemulax all night. Kristy had told Penn all about the green trees of her home, the fields of soft grass, and the shimmering lakes filled with cool water instead of smoldering ash. And Penn had told Kristy all about his favorite Garate pit, dragon traps, and the Sacred Throne of Stink. But as day began to break and the excitement of escaping started to fade, anxiety crept into Penn's thoughts. And fear.

"I don't know about this anymore..." Penn wasn't sure if it was the swaying of the rickety bridge, but suddenly he felt like he was going to barf. "Maybe I should go back home. Turn myself in. Maybe they'll forgive me if I just explain..."

As much as Penn wanted to see and hear, and mostly smell, the lovely things Kristy talked about (if they were even real), it was starting to sink in—he'd just run away from everything and everyone he knew. He wouldn't be able to hide from Grabagorn Prime forever. Penn would be hunted and, once found, punished. He'd be forced to live in the dungeon pit. And what had it all been for? To help some strange women who had probably tricked him with the promise of a magical cure? For all he knew, Lemon Bubbles didn't even exist. They sounded pretty fake, now that he thought about it.

"What am I doing?" Penn stopped walking across the cables and spun around. "I have to get out of here." Kristy ran right into him and nearly fell into the ash lake. But Penn's reflexes were fast, and he was able to steady her. "This is a total disaster, Kristy. I should never have listened to you! Are Lemon Bubbles even real? I bet they're not! I bet you and your womenfolk friends MADE THEM UP!"

Anger swirled inside him. Why couldn't he control it? He held on to the hot cable with his hands, not even caring if they got scorched. But instead of burning, he could see that now both his hands were blue and hairy! "Nooo!" he wailed. He looked into her eyes. Kristy and the women had ruined everything! "This. Is. Your. Fault!"

But Kristy didn't yell back. It was strange. Instead, she bowed her head. "I'm so, so, so sorry. I didn't mean to make you sad."

Penn felt more hot yelling rising up in him, like when you barf, then feel better, then barf again. "I'm not sad, Kristy. I'm *mad! Okay?!*"

"Okay, okay." She stepped back. "I'm sorry."

Was it Penn's imagination or was Kristy looking pale? Her eyes filled with a familiar expression of guilt and sadness. Penn knew that feeling. He felt it every time Grabagorn Prime yelled at him for forgetting to do his daily chin-ups or doodling pictures on his napkin at Night Meal or asking about his parents. He'd been told they were both killed in the Great Scorch.

"It's okay," Penn said with a huge sigh. He forced himself to shake off his anger. "But what do we do now?"

"We get the heck off this scary bridge, out of North Greemulax, and straight to those Lemon Bubbles!" Kristy's face broke into a smile as she edged past him and practically skipped the rest of the way to the other side.

Penn took a deep breath and followed her.

5

THE LEGEND OF
THE APPLE CORE

When they reached the wall, Penn remarked that it was much shorter than the section of the wall by the village. That part was tall and menacing and made of twisty iron with spikes on the ends. This section was made of splintery, loose planks of wood.

"I wonder why you guys built the wall to begin with," Kristy said.

"The elders wanted to keep dragons out," Penn said.

Or they wanted to keep you in, she thought but didn't say.

Kristy pried a nail out of a piece of wood, swung it aside, and walked right through. She assumed that Penn was close behind and turned to talk to him, but he was still on the other side, looking shocked.

"That was easy," was all he said as he finally stepped forward.

"Welcome to West Greemulax," Kristy announced with pride. She spun around, arms out, and her rainbow skirt twirled around her hips. "Isn't it beautiful?"

"Whoa. Everything you told me about— the fields of tall, green grass, the glittering streams, and the singing birds—it's all real!"

"Of course it's real!"

"And the sky is even blue!" He ran over to a patch of bright yellow flowers and yanked them from the dirt. He brought them to his nose and inhaled deeply. He sneezed.

Kristy laughed. "So what do you think?"

"It's so . . . colorful," Penn managed to squeak. "And the trees—they're covered in tiny green things."

He looked happy, truly happy, for the first time since they'd met. And that made Kristy happy. But these were just trees, and that was just sky, so it also made her a little sad to think about what life in North Greemulax was like.

Kristy led the way through the field and to a stream flanked by fruit trees. She knelt down and cupped her hands, filling them with cool water. Penn did the same.

"Even the water is better here," he said. "It tastes cool and clean."

After they drank, Kristy jumped up and plucked two apples from the nearest branch. She tossed one to Penn.

"What do I do with this?" he asked. "Throw it?"

"No, silly. It's an apple. You eat it!"

"Huh. I've never seen a tree with meat on it."

Kristy laughed again. "That's not meat, it's fruit. Four out of five worms recommend!"

He watched Kristy bite into her apple and did the same. "Wow," he said. "That's good."

They ate as they walked, crunching happily. Kristy told Penn all about the bad luck that had brought their mission to a crash-landing in North Greemulax. It had been her first outing in the trolley as a Rainbow Knight. It was only meant to be a routine flyover, where the Rainbow Knights scan the land below to make sure everything looks okay. As Rainbow Knights, they had all sworn to protect the vulnerable.

Kristy had been looking forward to her first trolley outing for weeks.

"I couldn't wait for Jackelion and X to show me the ropes, and afterward, we were supposed to get cake sandwiches to celebrate."

"What's a cake sandwich?"

"Two cakes with a cake in between. But then..."

"You got trapped instead," Penn said. He turned away, like he couldn't bear to look at her, then he changed the subject. "Are you going to get in trouble for jumping off the trolley?"

"I don't know," Kristy said. "Probably. I just hope they don't kick me out of the Knights. I love being a Rainbow Knight! But I couldn't leave you behind. Rainbow Knights are supposed to help people." She bent down and plucked one of her favorite things from the path. "A dandelion," she said happily.

"What's that?"

"You've never seen a dandelion before?"

He shook his head.

"You can wish on it."

"Wish on it? How?" he asked.

"Here, look." She closed her eyes, and after a few seconds she blew into it. She opened her eyes to see Penn watching as it broke into a hundred floaty bits of wish.

"That's the coolest thing I've even seen," Penn said, taking his last bite of apple, his hand now empty.

"Penn? Did you eat the whole apple? Like, the core and the stem, too?"

"I did. Was I not supposed to? I didn't know!"

"Well, you might grow an apple tree in your stomach. But probably not," Kristy said. "But if you choke on any of the seeds, let me know. I'm trained in the Ham Lick maneuver."

According to everything she had been

taught, Kristy was supposed to be scared of Penn. But how could she be scared of someone who smiled at a dandelion and ate the whole apple because he didn't know better? X always told her that Grabagorns never listened and never changed. She said you couldn't even get them to talk about their feelings or wear sweaters or floss their teeth. But Penn listened to her, and Penn had changed a lot from the boy who had trapped them in the first place.

Maybe he'd get the importance of flossing if she explained it to him slowly.

THE LEGEND OF HIGH FIVE

When they passed an oddly shaped bush for the third time, Penn stopped. "Kristy...this looks familiar. Are you sure we're on the right path to the Lemon Bubbles?"

"Let me see." Kristy licked a finger and held it up to the air. She narrowed her eyes as she decided what her readings had meant.

"Interesting. Very interesting." Kristy pulled out her compass and her Rainbow Knight map. After a moment of inspection, she folded the map back up.

Penn raised his eyebrows, hopeful. "Well?"

"I have a confession to make." Kristy winced. "I don't exactly know where to find Lemon Bubbles. I've never . . . um . . . seen one."

"YOU WHAT?!" Penn hollered. He felt a vein bulge in his forehead. She'd been leading him across the entirety of Greemulax, and she didn't even know where to find a Lemon Bubble?! "Why didn't you tell me?!" Penn said, throwing his arms up and noticing, for the first time, that his elbows looked much larger than usual. A little more blue in color, as well. "Not my elbows! They're my favorite part of my arms!"

"I'm so sorry, Penn!" Kristy collapsed into a pile of soft green grass. She hunched over and covered her face with her hands. Her voice was muffled as she spoke through them. "I thought I could just find a Lemon Bubble right away. I'm usually great at finding stuff. I'm sorry." Kristy's hands began to dull. Her red hair was looking grayish orange.

Even though he was having his own personal blue-elbow crisis, Penn was concerned about the changes. "Kristy, something weird is going on—"

"Wait!" Kristy interrupted. She pulled her hands away from her face and jumped up. "I have an idea. We'll go to Lillibop." Her eyes shone with excitement and her hands and hair were back to normal. Maybe he had imagined it? "She'll know what to do! She knows everything!" Kristy paced back and forth, suddenly full of energy. "After my parents were..."

Kristy stopped. Penn had never seen her at a loss for words. And he knew that what she couldn't say was that her parents were dead. Probably killed in the Great Scorch, like his.

"After my parents were gone," Kristy started again, "Lillibop looked after me. She taught me all sorts of cool stuff, like how to tie my shoes and how to stand up to evil. I know she'll be able to help us."

As Kristy took off running into the lush forest, Penn realized he had no other option but to follow her. Perhaps this mysterious Lillibop would know something about Lemon Bubbles. In the meantime, Penn was going to have to try to stay calm.

It was a pretty long trek to the westernmost tip of West Greemulax, where Lillibop was rumored to have moved in order to live "off the grid" for a while and away from the rest of the women. Kristy told him Lillibop had relocated for some "alone time" and "self-care."

"I don't know what that is," Penn said.

"Me either!" Kristy laughed. "But it seems like something the wisers do with candles and comfy sweatpants."

He'd learned that "wisers" in the women's community were what he called "elders."

Penn laughed, too. Elders—and wisers, he guessed—were funny sometimes. He dutifully followed Kristy as she raced across the sunny paddocks and through shady forests. He quietly marveled at the dewy pine needles and red mushroom caps, along with lots of other little details that were waking up his senses. He hadn't realized the Man Caves had such a distinctive smell until he noticed the absence of it. A mustiness that reminded him of feet crossed with the odor of a wet bathing suit left overnight in a bag no longer filled his nose.

Now, when the breeze blew, something sweet and flowery traveled with it, and an image of his mother flashed in his mind. She had been gone so long that his memories were really daydreams he'd pieced together listening to the elders talk. Not a memory but a wish.

"Okay, we're definitely close." Kristy unlatched a pair of binoculars from her belt loop. There was an aqua-colored glitter K sticker on the side of them. She held them up to her eyes and craned her neck, scanning the treetops as they walked. "Tell me if you see a tugboat."

"Why would we see one in the trees?"

"All women live in tree houses, silly." Kristy laughed. She was clearly enjoying teaching Penn about everything. "And Lillibop's tree house is a sideways tugboat."

"But why?"

"Why not?"

They wove through the forest, searching every tree but finding zero tugboats. Kristy even climbed a few trees, just in case Lillibop had an invisibility tent over her tugboat. She counted her steps and licked her finger to determine the direction of the wind three more times.

"Does that work?" Penn wondered aloud.

Kristy looked wisely into the distance. "Well, truth be told, I just found a little maple syrup on my finger, so . . . it worked for that, yeah."

When they'd finally reached another grassy clearing, Penn could feel himself getting upset again. Had Kristy led them into another dead end?

"Just as I suspected," Kristy said with a satisfied nod as she surveyed the land in front of her. She began to jump up and down, elated. "It's a mobstacle course."

"A what?"

"A mobstacle course! A maze obstacle course. We have to walk through it to get to Lillibop's house. Brilliant."

Penn looked out to the field, confused. Every obstacle course he'd ever done had involved Garate-chopping random stuff and doing chin-ups, and had always ended with an eating contest. But here were tall hedges and twenty potential entranceways. "How do we know where to start?" he asked.

"The doors are all a different color."

Penn hadn't noticed that.

"So I think we have to find the right color," Kristy said as if it was the most obvious thing in the world, which he guessed to her it was.

"But how?"

"We have to listen."

Penn started to say that that made no sense, but Kristy put her finger to her lips in a "shush" motion. There was a noise, but it was barely audible. It sounded like birdsong. "I think we have to find where it's coming from!"

Penn and Kristy tiptoed to the different openings in the maze, listening. After the first three, Penn gave up. He plopped down on the grass, crossed his arms, and wondered what his life had come to. Kristy kept creeping around, cupping her ear. After stopping at ten of them, Kristy reached down into a patch of grass and triumphantly pulled out a purple plastic bird. "Found it!"

Penn rushed over, impressed. Was there nothing Kristy couldn't do? "Now what?"

"Now we go this way," she said, skipping to the purple door. They followed the twisty turns between the hedges until they came to a wooden pole about three feet off the ground, blocking their path.

"Is that for chin-ups?" he asked.

"No way, it's too low."

"I guess we're supposed to step over it, then," Penn said. He lifted his foot, but as soon as he grazed the top of the pole with his shoe, the pole zapped him. "Ouch!" he cried.

"No, silly," Kristy said. "You gotta limbo."

Penn had no idea what that meant, but he hoped it wouldn't hurt as much as the zapping.

"Like this." Kristy leaned back and shimmied and scooted under the stick without any part of her body touching it.

"Um, I'm not sure I can do that," he said.

"Of course you can," she said. "Give it a try."

He tried to lean back while worming his way under, but he fell down.

He imagined what Marcus, Brandon, and Landon would think if they could see him now. His cheeks burned with embarrassment. He pounded the ground with his monster paw.

Kristy started to say something, and without

even realizing it, he growled at her. At her startled look, he apologized but insisted she turn away so he could limbo in private. He was the most flexible of his friends—the only one who could touch his toes—so why couldn't he do this? After a few more failed attempts, he was ready to give up.

"Bend your knees," Kristy suggested, her back to him.

What did she know? he thought. On the other hand (paw?), she had made it through pretty easily.

He bent his knees as he leaned back and . . . it worked.

Finally!

"High five," Kristy said. Penn lifted his paw and clapped it together with her hand. He loved high fives. Kristy's huge grin told him she did, too.

They kept walking down the path. After

more twists and turns, they saw a large nest with three speckled blue eggs inside.

Were they supposed to eat them?

Penn was getting pretty hungry. All he'd consumed since yesterday was some apples and stream water.

Kristy sat next to the nest. She carefully took one of the eggs out and held it in her hand. "Oooh, it's warming up. I bet it's a waiting game," she said. "I activated it by touching it, and now we wait for it to hatch."

"How is waiting a game?" Penn asked.

Kristy shrugged and continued to wait.

A minute passed.

"How long will we have to wait?" Penn asked.

"I don't know," she said. "We'll have to wait and see."

Another minute passed.

"I'm tired of waiting," Penn grumbled.

"And I have a better idea. I'll hatch it." He picked up one of the eggs and threw it against the tree. It exploded into a puff of blue dust and sparkles.

"I don't think that worked," Kristy said with a sigh.

"HOOBASTANK!" Penn let out. His entire left arm began to pulse. A giant blue bicep tore through the sleeve of his shirt. It bulged out like a giant blueberry.

Kristy gasped at his disgusting arm and shook her head. "I got this," she said, settling in for a long staring contest with the egg in her hand. Only two minutes later, the shell popped open with an unceremonious, tiny *crack*. A shiny, golden key rose from the center. A curly letter *L* was engraved on it.

"I did it!" Kristy held the key up in the air like a trophy in one hand and raised her other up to Penn. "High five!"

"Great job," Penn offered, giving more of a low two. "You're much better at all these obstacles than I am."

"Don't feel discouraged," Kristy said in a slow, steady voice. "These obstacles were definitely designed with Rainbow Knights in mind. Lillibop's gotta keep Grabagorns out somehow. Besides, you did help me! You showed me what not to do. That was the most important part."

This made Penn feel much better. So why did Kristy look like she felt so much worse? As soon as the words had escaped her lips, the glow of Kristy's face seemed to fade. Penn was worried about her, but he didn't know what to do. Grabagorn Prime had obviously told some big lies, but it seemed like he wasn't wrong about Grabagorns needing to keep womenfolk safe. He could see that Kristy was suffering and needed his protection—from what, he wasn't sure.

THE LEGEND OF LILLIBOP

The outline of a door began to glow through the tree bark. When Kristy inserted the key into the glowing lock, it swung open to reveal a narrow, winding staircase. Kristy and Penn stepped inside, but Penn's monster arm kept scraping against the wall as they made the climb.

"Finally!" he whined, rubbing his blue

elbows once they reached the top. He stretched out into the extra space on the landing of Lillibop's tugboat.

The rest of Penn's grumpiness seemed to melt away as they looked around the warm home. It was spacious and cozy, with fabrics of every color and texture draped over the furniture. Large, cushy pillows covered in tassels and fringes were tossed around the floor. Golden vases stood on every table and wooden chest. A jeweled lamp hung from the ceiling, casting sparkles over all the room.

A gigantic rainbow-colored button hung at the center of the only white wall in the house. It begged to be pushed, and Kristy could see Penn fighting the impulse.

"You thinking about that rainbow button?" she asked.

"What? No." He looked away. "Yes. Can I push it?"

"Don't," she said. "Pushing other people's buttons is considered rude."

He nodded and clenched his paws together.

Kristy felt proud of his willpower. The wisers had always said that men were weak and irrational and controlled by anger, but she didn't think that was true for all of them. Sure, Penn got angry sometimes, and he wasn't great at climbing trees, but he was nice and thoughtful, and he was pretty good company, too.

"Can it be . . . ?" a high-pitched, breathy voice said from the shadows. "Is that my Kristy?" Lillibop stepped into the light. She had curly hair that looked like gold spaghetti, and it seemed as though she was wearing every piece of chunky jewelry in West Greemulax all at once. Her cheeks were rosy and her skin glowed. She looked exactly the same as Kristy remembered.

"It's me, Lillibop!" Kristy said, bursting

with joy. She ran over and embraced her old guardian. She had so much to tell her! It all came spilling out. "I've missed you so much. It's been quite an adventure getting here. See, I'm a Rainbow Knight now, and this is my friend, and we found him when we crash-landed in North Greemulax. It was a routine flyover, but Trolley 4 is *the worst*! Anyway, he needs—"

"He?" Lillibop gasped, hand to chest. She turned to Penn, noticing him for the first time. The rosy color drained from her face. "Kristy, dear . . . you brought this boy to my tugboat?" Kristy could see Lillibop's eyes dart to Penn's blue hands. He quickly put them behind his back, though the damage had already been done.

"Don't worry. This is Penn. He's a good one. He's trying *not* to become a Grabagorn." Kristy leaned in and whispered, "Although he's not doing the best job."

"Yes, so it appears," Lillibop replied. "Penn. It's nice to make your acquaintance." She tore her eyes away from him and excused herself for a minute. She invited Penn and Kristy to rest on the pillows. Kristy worried that she had upset Lillibop by bringing a boy to her tugboat.

As soon as they sat down, they melted into the soft fabric and at once felt completely rejuvenated, without even closing their eyes. Kristy had forgotten all about Lillibop's magical furniture. When Kristy was little, Lillibop had gifted her a stepping stool that let her reach anything, no matter how high it was. Kristy would use it to pluck the prettiest apples from the tops of the trees and bring them back home to make pie, coated in cinnamon and sugar.

"I didn't even know how tired I was until I sat down," Penn said. "Sorry for being such a grump, Kristy. I shouldn't have gotten so mad like that."

"It's totally okay, Penn," Kristy chirped. "You had a really long day."

Lillibop returned and headed for the kitchen. "Kristy, come here." Kristy obeyed, even though she was really enjoying sitting on the comfortable cushions. She didn't want to be rude. Lillibop handed Kristy a cup and saucer gilded with the crest of the Rainbow Knights. She looked at Penn, took a deep breath, and turned back to Kristy. "I don't like the way you're fading, dear. I can see through your ears. You got a whole lotta wax in there, by the way."

Kristy immediately put her hands to each side of her head. "What do you mean? I feel fine."

"You're being too accommodating. To me, to...this boy." Lillibop looked over at Penn, and her gaze lingered. "It's okay to get angry or annoyed, to be exhausted yourself sometimes." Lillibop led Kristy to a tall mirror propped against the wall.

When Kristy took in her reflection, she gasped. "You're right. My hair is dull and my skin is . . . fading?" She also still had some burrs in her hair and black ash on her boots, but that was neither here nor there.

"Now you see what I mean?" Lillibop asked.

Kristy nodded.

Then Lillibop gestured to Penn, who dozed quietly on his cushion. "How is he not full Grabagorn yet?"

"Because I've been helping him calm down." Kristy smiled. "Every time he starts to lose his temper, I remind him that's not who he is. His anger doesn't control him." She actually felt really good about that. She didn't like that Lillibop wanted her to be angry. Then she'd be no better than a Grabagorn! "Besides, I hate anger!" Kristy added, feeling angry.

"And Penn saved us from the pit. I owe it to him to help him. I promised."

"But you're disappearing." Lillibop rested a hand on Kristy's armored shoulder. "Once you let part of yourself disappear, it's not easy to get it back."

"You worry too much, Lillibop," Kristy assured her. "I'm not gonna, like, *stop existing*." She took a sip of her tea. "I'll totally figure that out *after* I help Penn find his Lemon Bubble." Kristy brightened, remembering their mission. "Which is exactly why we're here! Do you know where we can find some?"

"Lemon Bubbles?"

"Yeah," Kristy said. "We heard they help stop the Grabagorn process."

Lillibop nodded. "In the Forest of Candy, of course. I've heard a lot of different rumors. Most of the candies there have magical, mystical properties. But they're not always so predictable, the candies," Lillibop said, a note of concern in her voice. "I once ate some Curly Cubes to help me sleep, and I ended up sprouting a third eye that wouldn't go away for a couple days. And it was on my chin!"

Lillibop waved her hand, and the teapot rose into the air. It flew across the room and refilled Penn's and Kristy's teacups. Penn startled at the sound of his cup sliding on its saucer, and his jaw almost hit the cushion. Kristy giggled. Lillibop was showing off. "It's where I get my Sour Squishers. Unfortunately, my supply is running pretty low, so I can only do that sort of thing once in a while to impress guests." Lillibop grinned and raised her eyebrows hopefully. "Unless..."

"We could get some for you," Kristy said. "When we find Penn's Lemon Bubble."

"That would be so nice of you. Both of you," Lillibop said, still smiling.

Penn smiled back.

Kristy caught her own reflection again. She *did* seem less solid, especially her head. . . . She turned her attention back to Lillibop. "Do you think there's a candy that can help me?"

"Listen, both of you. Don't get greedy with the candy. You'll get Type I Diagreedies."

Kristy didn't know what that was, but she didn't want to find out.

"Magic candy is serious business," Lillibop continued, "and after you eat it, you might get sad and want more candy. But I don't care what you've been told—it's not a permanent fix."

"Thanks a lot, magic," Kristy sighed, rolling her eyes and flopping back onto the pillows. To add injury to insult, one of the spiky burrs in her hair poked her in the neck.

"Sorry, kid. If you need permanent help, you've got to do that on your own," Lillibop reminded her. "You can only shine on the outside if what's inside feels that way."

Kristy had heard that a million times, and she knew that before the Grape Escape a lot of women suffered from disappearing, but this was the first time she'd ever felt the slightest bit dull. She was also a little offended at the idea that her insides were anything but bright.

"The Forest of Candy is in South Greemulax," Lillibop said, leading the kids over to her wooden farm table. She pushed some bottles aside and rolled out a large piece of paper. Lillibop closed her eyes and began to dip brushes in paint with her mind, illustrating a beautiful map of all the Greemulaxes. She finished by painting a fearsome green dragon right near the Forest of Candy. "That's where the dragons live, too."

Kristy and Penn exchanged a look. They were both scared, but too proud to admit it. Kristy had seen a dragon at a distance once, when the wisers were meeting with one on diplomatic matters, but she'd never interacted with one. Although she was the best student in Madame Scruggs's Dragonese for Dames class.

"Don't worry," Penn said, summoning a little bravery, "I am a highly trained Garate fighter. I can protect you." He put his hands up in a chopping stance.

Kristy didn't want to hurt his feelings, but "garate" didn't sound very menacing. "It's too bad we can't use a trolley."

"This is an adventure that must be attempted on foot," Lillibop said. "Step by step. By step."

Once the map had dried and they'd been gifted two satchels for transporting candy, plus a fishing net—because you never know when a fishing net might come in handy, and when you live in a sideways tugboat, there's always a spare—Lillibop showed Penn and

Kristy to the back door, where they could avoid the mobstacle course.

She gave Kristy a big hug and it looked like she was going to hug Penn, too, but instead she awkwardly shook his paw. "Farewell, my little adventurers!" Lillibop said, waving to the Rainbow Knight and the Graba-boy as they set off toward the south. "Come back soon with those Sour Squishers! And remember: Remain careful, wise, and"—she looked at Kristy—"solid."

THE LEGEND OF THE SPOON IN THE ROAD

It had become clear pretty quickly that Lillibop's map wasn't exactly accurate. Either she'd taken some artistic license, or perhaps the landscape had changed. No matter the reason, Penn and Kristy had been walking for hours and hours and they were lost. *Hours* and *hours* and *hours*.

Currently, Kristy was sitting cross-legged on the grass with the map laid out in front of her. She was busy drawing a line through the path they'd taken. Rainbow Knights had glitter pens in their utility belts along with seemingly everything else. Penn was secretly impressed with how prepared Kristy was for . . . anything. But he was less than impressed with Lillibop's mapmaking skills. Penn scratched at the dirt, working hard not to get angry. He didn't need any more Grabagorn limbs, thank you very much.

"Ohhhh, *that's* where we went wrong." Kristy nodded. Her eyes remained fixed on the map. "We should have turned *left* at the Twisty Trees to get to the Happy Hills. And we weren't supposed to be looking for a fork in the road—it's a *spoon* that we want. Right near Pudding Lake." Kristy folded up the map and grinned. "Then we just cross it and *boom!* South Greemulax." She sprang to her feet and did a little victory dance. How was she so cheerful all the time?

"Spoon, not fork. Got it," Penn echoed in a monotone voice. He wondered where Kristy was getting all this endless energy. She had stopped fading, so maybe that was helping. "Okay, then. Lead the way."

The two retraced their steps back through the grove of Twisty Trees. Just like their name suggested, the tree branches looped and coiled around one another.

"Neato," Kristy said, stopping short. "Those trees look like they're hugging."

"What?" Penn said. "No way, they look like they're fighting each other. And the taller one is winning."

Kristy stared at him. "Umm, okay." Her cheeks flickered and faded, but she didn't seem to notice. She shook her head slightly at him and started walking again.

"What?" he said, trailing after her. "What did I say?"

She didn't respond. She'd been doing that all day. Silently judging him but pretending she wasn't. He did not like that.

After Penn and Kristy navigated the trail through the Twisty Trees, they hiked up and down the Happy Hills, feeling a strange sense of joy wash over them with each step. Happy hills were the best.

Next, they followed the road.

"Penn, look!"

"What?"

"It's the spoon in the road." She pointed in front of her to where the ground dipped into what felt like a large round bowl. "If you squint, it's totally a spoon. See? We're on the right track. Pudding Lake is after the handle."

Kristy skipped into the landmark.

And then she froze.

Penn caught up with her, and Kristy put a finger to her lips.

"Did you hear that?" Her eyes darted back and forth suspiciously.

"Hear what?" Penn replied, at full volume.

"Shhh!" Kristy hissed. She crept around, searching.

What now? he thought as he watched her. She was always stopping to chat, or to look up at a bird she thought was cool or try to talk to a squirrel that wanted nothing to do with her. It's a miracle that they'd made it this far.

"I felt the Neck Prickles," she said. "I think something is following us."

"All the way here? No way. You're imagining things." Penn's stomach let out a loud, angry noise.

"No need to growl at me!" Kristy barked. She crossed her arms over her chest and frowned as she caught a glimpse of her pale hands. *Was that a blue spot on her thumb?*

"That was my stomach!" Penn yelled, stomping his foot. When he was hungry, it was like his head could hold no other thoughts. "I'm starving. Why didn't Lillibop give us something to eat? Hurry up, let's keep moving."

"But, Penn, I feel like something—"

"Come on!" he yelled. "We can't keep stopping every time you have a FEELING!" Just then, his ear started to buzz. What the ham sandwich?

"Penn," she said slowly, stretching out the one syllable. "I don't want to alarm you, but...your ear is...well, it's big. And blue. And there are hairs growing out of it."

"Argh!" He swatted at his ear, but it continued to buzz. Plus he smelled that musty wet-bathing-suit-in-a-bag-overnight smell.

Penn suddenly felt so mad, he had to do something about it. He ran over to the nearest

tree and was about to kick it Roundpit-style when
he noticed blue Grabagorn feet next to the trunk.
He knew those feet. He knew that smell. Had they
always smelled like that? Did *he* smell like that?

"Landon? . . . Brandon?!" The blood drained
from Penn's face as the twins stepped out into
the bowl.

The boys stood tall, trying to look tough.
It worked.

This was it, Penn thought. Grabagorn
Prime was likely not far behind. Penn was
caught. But maybe he could buy himself some
time, or at least save Kristy. The thought surprised him but also gave him courage. "What
are you guys doing here?"

"Following a traitor," Brandon snarled.
As if it needed more explanation, he added,
"That's you, Penn. *You're* the traitor."

"Yeah!" Landon agreed. "That's what we
call traitors now: Penns!"

Penn was having trouble hearing because of the buzzing. But he heard that. "Hey, that's hurtful," he said.

"Well, it's a thing now," Brandon said. "That happened since you've been gone."

"And we're gonna be the ones to bring you back," Landon added.

"You guys are out here alone?" Penn asked.

"Yes. And we're going to get a sick reward for finding you."

Penn breathed a quiet sigh of relief. He could handle Brandon and Landon on their own.

"You better explain what's going on!" Landon said. "Why did you set the women free?"

"And why did you go with them?" Brandon asked.

"We don't understand why."

"We're very confused."

Penn looked at his friends, then back at Kristy, and realized the only thing he could say was the truth that he'd known for a while but hadn't understood. "I don't want to be a Grabagorn," he explained.

"What?"

"Why?"

"Because I don't want to be a monster."

"But . . ." Brandon said.

"What else could we be?" Landon added.

Penn shrugged. "I want to stay me." He heard Kristy's quiet-but-loud *yes* behind him.

The twins stared at him a moment, then both started laughing.

"Dude, you had us going for a minute."

"We'll cover for you," Landon said. "Just come with us and bring the tiny woman."

"Yeah, we'll tell Grabagorn Prime that she escaped and you've been trying to catch her this whole time. You'll be a hero," Brandon said. "I mean, we'll be the bigger heroes for finding you, but we'll let you take some of the credit. By the way, your arm looks awesome." The twins took turns poking at Penn's blue bicep.

"So big," Landon said.

"So blue," Brandon added.

"But I don't want to go back." Penn put his hands to his head. The buzzing in his ear hadn't gone away, and somehow the arrival of Brandon and Landon was making it worse. He had to work extra hard to listen to them. Penn looked back and forth between his old friends and his new one. He didn't want to be a Grabagorn. He knew this now. He also knew that he could keep saying it to Brandon and Landon until he was blue in the face (oh, is that where that saying came from?), and they wouldn't understand. "I want to go with Kristy. I want a chance to be . . . better. Please, just go home. Pretend you never saw us."

Landon shook his head. "We can't do that."

Penn stared at Landon. Landon stared at

Brandon. Brandon was staring at something on his own foot.

"Run to Pudding Lake!" Penn yelled to Kristy as he shoved Landon into Brandon and watched them fall over in a heap. Then he took off in the same direction.

"You were great back there!" Kristy shouted when Penn caught up to her.

"Thanks!" he yelled back, speeding down the spoon-handle road.

When they reached the end, she called out, "To the left!"

As the two turned the corner, they were met with the oddest sight. A steep cliff's edge overlooked a round lake of thick, yellow... pudding? This must be Pudding Lake, just like the map had said. Penn guessed it was hard to misplace a whole lake of pudding. He barely had time to register what was in front of him before he felt Kristy grab his hand, say, "I knew the wisers were wrong about boys! I knew you could change if you wanted to!" and jump, pulling him off the ledge along with her.

Splat! The thick goop broke their fall.

Up above, Landon and Brandon skidded to the edge of the cliff. They looked to the left and to the right in confusion and then looked down.

"There they are!" Landon cried.

"Kristy?" Penn flung his arm out to reach for her, and a huge glob of pudding landed directly in his mouth. Oh, wow. "Try the pudding! It's delicious!"

"It sure is," Kristy said as she took a bite. "It has banana chunks in it!"

"Should we jump in after them?" Brandon asked.

"I guess," said Landon.

"We have to get out of here," Penn said. He flailed around in slow motion, struggling to move his limbs through the gooey pudding.

"For sure," Kristy said. "But where do we—"
Before she could finish her sentence, Kristy's
head disappeared under the gloop with a loud
smacking noise and a few pudding bubbles.

"Kristy!" Penn cried out. He was about
to dive in after her, when he felt something
tug at his leg. He took a deep breath and shut
his eyes just as something pulled him under,
sticky pudding covering his face. Sticky pudding closing out the sky above him.

9

THE LEGEND OF THE PUDDING MAN

Penn felt himself being pulled down, down, down. He kept his eyes and mouth closed so the lake of dessert wouldn't blind or choke him, but the pudding definitely got into his nose.

Who—or what—was pulling him? Where was it taking him?

After what seemed like forever but also only a second, Penn heard and kind of felt a loud *sluuuuurrrrrpp* noise, and then he hit the ground. He looked around and saw that they were in a room.

"Ahhhhhh!" Penn and Kristy yelled in unison, gasping for air. They were lying on a wooden floor that was painted in a bright daisy pattern. Penn traced the petals with his pudding-covered fingers, trying to make sense of where he was.

"Children!" A loud, singsongy voice cut through Penn's haze. "Are you okay?! I'm so sorry I had to pull you down like that without asking first!"

Penn wiped the pudding from his eyes and sat up. He was met with a sight that was both peculiar and wonderful: It was a grown man . . . and he was *not* a Grabagorn!

"I didn't want those grabagoons to catch

you," he said. The man was tall, with a dark complexion like Penn's and kind eyes. He wore vibrant purple pants and a paisley-patterned shirt of rainbow colors that was bedazzled with the word *Turdgon*. The man licked a glob of pudding splatter off his arm and reached out to Penn and Kristy.

"Why does your shirt say *Turd gun*?" Penn asked, grabbing onto the man's hand and pulling himself to his feet. He tried not to giggle.

"Excuzay you! It's pronounced Tur-*jon*!" Turdgon said in a French accent, hand to his chest. "And it's my name. Turdgon, the Pudding Man."

"It sounds fancy," Kristy said. "Nice to meet you, Tur-Jon. My name's Kristy and this is Penn." She wrung out her hair, and pudding rained onto her boots. "And I'm very impressed by Pudding Lake. It smells great and tastes like bananas—"

"Plantains, babygirl," Turdgon corrected. He motioned to Penn and Kristy to follow him. "Let's get you cleaned off." He led them into a cozy room shaped like a dome. "Just step through the washtube."

He stepped through first and Penn followed. The ceiling was a big skylight, offering an under-pudding view. Before Penn knew what was happening, a spray of water covered his face and clothes, and then soap, and then more water, and then his entire body was blow-dried.

"Wow!" he said, stepping into the next room.

"It's a human trolley wash," Turdgon said with a smile. "Cool, huh?"

Penn heard a thump from the washtube ceiling, so he stepped back and looked up to see a very fat polka-dot fish staring at him. The fish looked dazed. It shook it off and swam-waddled away.

"Fluffing amazing!" Kristy said, when she stepped out of the washtube.

This room had a small dining alcove in the corner. On the table, there was a bowl of fresh pudding covered in frilly swirls of whipped cream along with rainbow sprinkles, chocolate sauce, and bright red cherries.

"Yummy!" Kristy exclaimed. It had been so long since they'd eaten. Even though they had just been covered in the stuff, the pudding still looked scrumptious. Penn and Kristy slid into the booth as Turdgon served them. They dug in. It tasted even better than when they were swimming in it.

"So what brings you two to Pudding Lake?" Turdgon moved about, bringing more snacks to the table. "Why were you being chased? Who was trying to snatch you?! Tell me all the things!"

"Well, we've been on an adventure," Kristy

explained. She patted Penn's blue shoulder. "Penn here rescued me and my fellow Rainbow Knights from a Grabagorn pit!"

Turdgon grabbed Kristy's hand. "What were you doing in North Greemulax?" His eyes went wide and then darted to Penn. "And you're a North Greemulax escapee? That explains the Grabagorn hands and ear, then."

Penn hid his hands in his lap and bowed his head. He still hated the ugly things. He couldn't hide his good-for-nothing ear, though. "I've already started to transformate—"

"But he doesn't want to!" Kristy interrupted. She smiled warmly at Penn. "He's different."

"So was I." Turdgon nodded his head. "That's why I escaped North Greemulax when I was your age."

"You did? How? Did you find the Lemon

Bubble?" Penn wanted to ask a million questions all at once. He concentrated on listening, so he could hear the answers.

Turdgon held his finger up to signal that he needed a moment and disappeared into the other room.

Suddenly, a set of red velvet curtains closed as if Penn and Kristy were the only guests at an exclusive dinner theater show. The lights dimmed and a low, sorrowful tune began to play. The curtains opened and a spotlight appeared. Turdgon stepped into it, wearing a shimmery blue cape trimmed in brown fur. His big eyes were filled with despair. He started singing:

"As a boy, he knew he had to flee.

He felt the monster inside him, you see.

But he didn't want to turn all the way blue.

There was a *glimmer* of a *glow* in there, too!"

Turdgon continued to sing the story of how he escaped North Greemulax, delivering each line with flourish and flair. Turdgon had been raised in North Greemulax, long before the Great Scorch. He'd always preferred to spend his days with the women rather than fighting and hanging out in the Man Caves with most of the other boys. He felt safe there, like he belonged. He could be strong, but he could also be sensitive and silly and completely fabulous. A few of the other boys also preferred to spend their time away from the caves, and Turdgon soon became best friends with a boy named Mandora. They spent their days singing songs, sewing clothes, and being friendly with the Grabagorns inside them but ignoring them when they got too monstery.

But the older men thought that all boys should embrace and feed their inner Grabagorn and let it take over. They separated Turdgon and the other boys from their mothers and sisters, except at mealtimes. Turdgon was miserable. He missed his friends and he hated being forced to fight all day.

So when Turdgon overheard the women planning the Grape Escape, he raced to find Mandora. Then the two boys hatched their own plan. They were going to escape, too! They knew not to drink the grape juice that fateful night, so they would dump theirs into the dirt. When all the other men fell asleep, they would follow the women. They would never be ruled by their monstery sides again.

"So they did!" Turdgon did a little twirl and posed, delivering his last stanza.

"Turdgon and Mandora lived happily ever after,

Having escaped from a life of disaster.

Loving their lair below the Pudding Lake,

A sparkly life they did maaaayayayayy-aaaaake!"

The last word hung in the air for a moment. Then Turdgon dipped into a deep bow. The curtains closed and the spotlight went out. Penn and Kristy stood, erupting into applause.

"That was brilliant!" Kristy said, smiling from ear to ear.

Turdgon reappeared, without his blue cape. "Thank you. I *do* love a good one-person show."

"Where's Mandora?" Kristy asked. "Can we meet him?"

"Oh, no, Ginger, Mandora's at work. He's a candystruction worker. You know the Marzipan Dam? He made that."

While Turdgon and Kristy talked about where Mandora was, Penn tried to clean himself up. The washtube was clearly not made for Grabagorns. His hairy Grabagorn hands were now crusted with dried pudding. He found the sink.

As Penn tried to scrub the crispy bits off,

the smell hit him and he suddenly remembered something strange. It was a small nagging thought, bubbling to the surface from somewhere deep. "Being covered in this stuff kinda reminds me of a dream I used to have all the time when I was younger," he said. He glanced over his shoulder. Turdgon and Kristy were now rapt with attention.

"I love it when people tell me their dreams," Kristy said. "Were you flying? Or were you in your room but it didn't look like your room, but you still knew it was your room? Or did you get an A+ on your history homework?"

Penn continued. "I was swimming, but the water was really... *goopy* or something. And everything around me looked huge. Or I was really tiny... and there was a woman carrying me through the goopy water. I think it was a woman. Then, out of nowhere... a monster would grab me!"

Turdgon gasped through a bite of pudding. Some sprinkles fell out onto his chin. "What happened next?!"

Penn shrugged. "I don't know. I always woke up at that part. Pretty weird, huh?"

"That sounds a lot like Pudding Lake," Kristy said. "Doesn't it, Tor-zhawn?" She made the name sound extra French.

Turdgon nodded in agreement. "I know pudding when I hear about it," he replied. "And I'm sorry to tell you this, but I believe your dream was based on real life."

"But how? I've never been to Pudding Lake until today." Penn's neck began to feel prickly, like Kristy had described before. It didn't feel good. "Have I?"

"Oh, you poor child!" Turdgon cried. He sprang forward and pulled Penn into a big bear hug. Penn's face squished into the paisley fabric of Turdgon's shirt. So this was a hug? Weird. It was like a chest bump, but didn't feel as lame. He relaxed into it. "It's a shame that you have to hear this from Turdgon, since I can't stand telling people sad things. But...during the Grape Escape, some of the women tried to swim across Pudding Lake with their baby sons. They wanted to save them from growing up in a place that didn't let them be their whole selves, but Grabagorn Prime's goons...well, they wouldn't let that happen. They followed the women and ripped the little babies from their arms!" Turdgon let out a huge, dramatic sob.

Kristy caught Penn's eye as Turdgon released him. Penn was frozen.

Kristy passed Turdgon a pink velvet hankie. He sniffed loudly. "Thank you. Giving bad news is exhausting!" He leaned on Kristy as he lowered himself back into his chair. "Don't make me do it again, kids."

Kristy whispered to Penn, "I'm so sorry."

"Don't be sorry!" Penn exclaimed. "That wasn't bad news. It was amazing news. It was the best news I've ever heard." He stood up straighter. In fact, Penn felt as if he would float off into the sky if he wasn't beneath a lake of plantain-flavored dessert right now.

"But how, child?" sniffed Turdgon. "I just told you that you were ripped from your mother's arms." He sobbed again.

"Exactly. And that means she could still be alive!" Penn ran over to Kristy. He didn't want to waste another moment. "Come on! We have to go find those Lemon Bubbles right now. If I transformate into a full Grabagorn before we find her, she might never recognize me."

"Good point," Turdgon said.

"Very good point," Kristy agreed. "We have to trolley on out of here. Or at least swim."

Turdgon checked his puddinscope to make sure Brandon and Landon were no longer lurking around, then quickly packed up some provisions and handed them *Dum Dum's Guide to the Forest of Candy*, *Updated Edition*. "I've heard that rumor about Lemon Bubbles. It hasn't made it to *Dum Dum* yet, though. But I believe in candy."

Turdgon showed Penn and Kristy how to avoid the pudding and get out through a tunnel.

"Thank you for your help," Kristy said.

"You're the best," Penn said. "And—"

"Oh, stop," he said, waving away their compliments.

Penn stopped.

"No, no, no, figure of speech, keep going," Turdgon said, shimmying his shoulders.

"Thank you for telling me the truth about my dream. When I was a kid I asked the older Grabagorns what my dream meant, and they just told me to do more Garate so I'd sleep harder and stop having dumb dreams."

Turdgon patted his head awkwardly. "You're still a kid."

Penn sniffled and looked away. "Is there anything you want from the Forest of Candy?" he asked. He thought it was only polite to offer, after everything Turdgon had done for them.

"Well, if you don't mind . . . Mandora and I do love those Fudgy Finches. They make you fly! We tried them once and it was a real hoot. We raced the trolleys but crashed one into a—" Turdgon stopped himself. "Actually, you don't need to know that part."

"One bag of Fudgy Finches coming right up!" Kristy said, pulling out her map. "Thanks again, Turgaloo!" She skipped ahead, clearly feeling happy now that they were full of yummy pudding and on their way again. But Penn had only taken a few steps before Turdgon caught up with him.

"Penn, wait! Be careful in South Gree-mulax. Those dragons are scary. And while they are on decent terms with the womenfolk community, they do *not* like people in general. Especially part-Grabagorns!" Turdgon shuddered at the thought of it.

"Will do." Penn gave the Pudding Man a nod and a salute to reassure him. But deep down, Penn was scared. Of the dragons. Of the Grabagorns. And of not getting to the Lemon Bubbles in time. He wanted to meet his mother. He just hoped it wasn't too late to find her.

10

THE LEGEND OF DRAGONS

The map was looking a little worse for wear after being drenched in all that pudding, but at least Kristy and Penn had finally crossed over into South Greemulax.

"I think we're almost there!" Kristy pointed to the paper to show Penn the route they'd been walking. She traced her finger along the green path, past the stained dragon, and over to the picture of Lollicrunchies and Peppermint Pops sticking out of the grass. "See? The Forest of Candy awaits!"

"Really? That's great," Penn said absent-mindedly. Ever since Turdgon had suggested that Penn's dream was real, Kristy could tell Penn was nervous. It was sweet how excited he was to look for his mother. As an orphan herself, Kristy had always longed for her parents. She understood.

They crept along the path as quietly as possible. According to Kristy's Rainbow Knight handbook, dragons had a horrible sense of smell (due to all that constant fire and smoke). As long as she and Penn didn't make any noise, maybe the dragons wouldn't even notice that they were nearby.

Everything was going perfectly until Penn whispered, "Oh no."

Kristy looked back to see what was wrong.

"I have to boof," Penn said.

Kristy didn't know what that meant.

"All that pudding," Penn explained. "I have to rip one."

"Oh, you have to toot?"

"Toot?" He laughed a little, and then a look of alarm crossed his face and he forced himself to stop.

"Can't you hold it?" Kristy whispered fiercely.

"Boys are born without that muscle. We learned about it in Fart Class."

"I think we call that Biology. And that is not true." Kristy sighed and shook her head. "I never thought I'd say this, but come on, Silent but Deadly. Come on, Silent but Deadly."

Kristy could see that Penn was concentrating hard to let his gas out flat and sideways. But it got away from him, and right at the end he let out a high-pitched *fffffffyorp* that sounded like someone letting go of a balloon.

Penn giggled and high-fived himself out of habit. Then he remembered to be scared.

Kristy and Penn froze in place.

Silence.

Then: *"RRRROOOAAAARRR!"* The growl boomed through the forest as the air began to smell of burning wood. The dragons had heard them. There was no time to make another plan. They just had to find cover—fast.

"Penn!" Kristy yelled as she darted through the trees. "Hide!"

"But only a Grabagorn can beat a dragon!" Penn yelled back as a fireball careened toward his left shoulder.

"You're not a full Grabagorn yet!"

"I've been preparing for this moment my whole life," he panted. He spun around and held his hands in a Garate stance, but the seat of his pants was already on fire. "Ahhhh!" Penn screamed, trying to put the flames out against a mossy tree trunk.

"Just hide!" Wow, maybe Graba-boys really were as dense as X said they were. Kristy scanned ahead for a cave or a boulder, or *anything* to crouch under. But all she saw were spindly trees that provided little cover. Kristy glanced quickly over her shoulder as she ran, but Penn was gone.

The dragons growled again, breathing fire onto the treetops as they swooped down. Kristy could feel the heat on the top of her head, but she didn't look up. She just kept running.

By the time she reached a clearing in the woods, she was trapped. Dragons were approaching from every direction! Except they looked much smaller than she thought they would—about the size of a cute pony. But they were still scary with their shimmering scales, big, big yellow eyes, and pointy teeth. And the flames-pouring-out-of-their-faces thing.

Kristy jumped behind the largest tree trunk she could find and crouched down low, watching the dragons as they landed one by one and stood in a circle. There were five of them. They seemed to be calming down from their fiery outburst, but Kristy had every intention of staying where she was until they went away. She spotted Penn by another tree and motioned for him to get low. They just needed to keep quiet, and everything would be fine. They'd be back on the path to Lemon Bubbles in no time.

"Stay back, dragons!" Penn shouted as he ran out into the clearing. "Or I'll Roundpit you!" He spun around really fast, then ran forward and kicked the air with a grunt. He looked like a dog chasing its tail and then giving up. These were the famous Garate moves that would supposedly defeat a dragon?

The dragons just looked at him, and one of them started making a high-pitched "Hee-hee-*rawr*" sound. Kristy covered her ears. Then the rest of the dragons joined in.

"Hee-hee-*rawr*! Hee-hee-*rawr*! Hee-hee-*rawr*!" One doubled over, then leaned on another in a familiar way.

Oh.

Oh!

Kristy realized they were *laughing*. At Penn.

Then one of them, the smallest one, shook her head and started to cry.

What was happening?

Kristy tried to remember what she could from Madame Scruggs's Dragonese class. It was worth a try.

Kristy stepped out from behind her tree

and approached a small turquoise dragon with long eyelashes. She tapped her on the tail. *"Roar roar...roaar roarrr?"*

Before the dragons could respond, Penn yanked Kristy back behind a tree. He shielded her with his arms. "What are you doing? And what did you say to them?"

"I asked them if they were okay."

"Let me handle this—I'm the one who is trained in dragon combat!" Past Penn's head, Kristy could see that the dragons still hadn't moved, but she thought she saw the turquoise one crying, too.

"I know why they're so small. They're *baby* dragons, Penn!" Kristy pushed past him. "Awwww."

Penn furrowed his brow. He looked very Grabagorny when he did that. "How do you know? And even if they are, baby dragons are still dragons."

"I just know, and I think they need our help." Kristy jogged out to the center of the baby dragon circle and tried again. She pointed to herself and said her name in Dragonese. *"Rrroar!"*

"Ror roarr roar rroar!!" one of the dragons sniffled. *"Roar ro-oar?"*

Kristy nodded as if she understood. In truth, her Dragonese was rusty, so she could only pick out a few words.

"What are they saying?" Penn asked, still eyeing the brood suspiciously. He started to pace back and forth. He seemed annoyed. It was only a matter of time before more of his body parts would start turning blue. Now that she'd gotten used to it, Kristy didn't find the blue so scary anymore. It was actually kind of cool.

"I think they lost their parents!" Kristy said. If anyone knew what it was like to lose their parents, it was Kristy and Penn. How lucky that they had been the ones to meet the baby dragons! Kristy knew what had to be done. She took her powerful Rainbow Knight stance, feet shoulder-width apart and hands on hips. "Penn, we have to help these babies find their parents."

"Find adult dragons?" Penn asked. "On purpose? Weren't we just running for our lives a second ago? We're already on our way to the Forest of Candy. Remember? Lemon Bubbles? We don't have time to help dragons."

"There's always time to help the vulnerable, Penn," Kristy reminded him. "Haven't you ever heard of the Power of One? If you help just one person...you help the whole world!" It didn't matter that they weren't people; dragons were definitely included in this equation, too.

"I thought I was the person," Penn muttered to himself.

"Don't worry, babies." Kristy skipped over to the cutest, tiniest dragon. She was yellow with gold spots on her back scales. "We'll take you to your parents. Sorry—I mean, *roarrr ro-oar!*" At this, the dragons began to jump and flap their wings with delight.

A purple baby dragon stomped over and nuzzled Penn in gratitude. The boy regarded the dragon suspiciously but couldn't help petting him on the head. "You are pretty cute. Even if you did burn a hole in the butt of my pants."

"Are you sure you didn't do that from the inside when you *boofed*?" Kristy zinged.

Penn laughed. "Fine, Kristy, let's go find some dragons."

For the next hour, Penn and Kristy kept to the path that was supposed to lead to Dragon

Town, which was only a little out of the way to the Forest of Candy. The dragons walked in front of them, eating leaves from the over-hanging branches along the path, clearing the way for Penn and Kristy to walk. Kristy thought it was pretty fun!

But Penn seemed anxious, and his anx-iousness was seeping into Kristy's mood like lake pudding. As they walked, Kristy used a whole bunch of her energy to figure out what could be making Penn mad. She knew he was not thrilled about this detour. But maybe Penn was also still having a hard time letting go of the whole "Great Scorch" thing. She understood—when you've been told something your whole life, it was hard to accept that it wasn't true. But maybe he was warming up to the Power of One. She bet he would feel great about it when the babies were reunited with their parents. It felt so good to help others.

"Does it seem like there are a lot of trees here?" Kristy wondered aloud. "You know, for burny dragonlands? Maybe we should stop and look at the map again." Just ahead, the trail split off into two directions.

"No, I remember the way to go," Penn insisted, pulling his water bottle out of his satchel and taking a big swig. "Definitely to the right."

Kristy was pretty sure that Penn was wrong. She started to unfold the map, but Penn put his big blue hand on it. "I'm *positive* that I'm right," he said.

Kristy didn't want to start a fight or anything, so they continued on to the right side of the trail.

But a few minutes later, the nagging feeling that they'd made a wrong turn would not go away. Kristy made the baby dragons stop while she retrieved the map from her satchel. "Penn,

I think maybe you're wrong?" Kristy wondered why that had come out as a question when she meant it as a regular sentence. She tried again. "Penn, I think maybe you're wrong?" Huh, her voice went up again. That was weird.

"I'm not wrong!" Penn huffed. "I'll show you. Give me that!" He tore the map from Kristy's hands.

That was a big no-no. Kristy had been polite and patient with him, but she was reaching her limit. "Will you just listen to me?!" Kristy shouted as she jumped onto the nearest boulder. A little extra height always made her feel powerful. "I knew we were supposed to go to the left, but I was trying to be nice, Penn! But the fact is you're going the wrong way!" As Kristy spoke up, the color came back to her cheeks and light began to dance on her skin.

"*Rrroar! Rrroar!*" The dragons cheered, pointing their claws at her in awe.

"Do I have something on my face? What is it, a bug?" Kristy touched her face and looked down at her hands. They were solid. And her skin was even brighter than before! "I'm back!"

"Okay," Penn sighed, looking at the map. "You *were* right. I guess I...I should have listened to you." The words hung in the air for a moment. Kristy liked the sound of them.

"Whoa!" Penn gasped. He put his hand to his ear. "The buzzing stopped! The buzzing stopped! Yes!" He raised his hand and she gave him a high five.

But a thought nagged at her. "Why?" she asked.

"Why what?"

"Why did it stop? Why now?"

"Who cares why! Why do you always have to question everything?" He skipped ahead of her, singing, "The buzzing is gone, the buzzing is gone, bye-bye buzzing..."

She and the dragons followed in his path.

Was it possible that it was because he had listened to her? It seemed clear that the angrier he got, the more Grabagorny he became. What if the nicer he was, the more human he stayed? Hmm. "Penn—"

"Everyone turn right here," Penn said, interrupting her as they arrived at the next fork in the road.

Kristy shook her head and pointed to the map. "No, Penn."

"That's the way to the Forest of Candy," he said.

"I know," she said. "But according to the map, Dragon Town is to the left. And I promised to help the babies find their parents."

"We'll do that after," he grumbled. "I promise, okay?"

"I promised I would do it now."

"I said no," he said. He tried to cross his

arms, but they were too big. So he hung them at his sides instead, his hands balled into frustrated fists.

"*No?*" Was he being serious? Did he not remember what just happened five minutes earlier? She stomped her boot on the ground. The baby dragons all stopped and looked at her. "You are not in charge!"

"I should be!" he said. "Grabagorns are supposed to be in charge! Men are good at maps, which is why they never have to ask for directions!"

Was he just spouting nonsense now?

"You're supposed to LISTEN TO ME! And besides, you would still be trapped in that pit if I hadn't saved you!" Now Penn pounded his foot into the dirt angrily. It kicked up a giant cloud of dust. By the time the dust settled, Penn's right foot had transformed! It looked hideous.

Disappointment flooded over her. Kristy had so wanted the wisers to be wrong about boys and men. She felt stupid to have been so full of hope. But she knew what she had to do.

"Okay, Penn, your thing is more important. We'll do your thing first." As the words left her mouth, she felt a chill. Her lips felt tingly and her cheeks felt cool.

"Okay!" Penn said. He was fixated on his new foot, which had burst right out of his shoe.

"Rooaar roahr roar rrroar," she told the dragons, assuring them she'd take care of them after they helped Penn. The chill in her cheeks drifted up to her forehead. When she touched her face, it felt clammy. Was she getting sick? But she got the flu shot this year!

"Um, Kristy?" Penn said, when he finally looked up at her. "Your head is sort of . . . invisible."

"Invisible how?"

"Like I can see through where your head was."

Kristy looked at her reflection in a nearby puddle, and sure enough, her head was gone.

"Fluffernutter!" she said. "That can't be good."

THE LEGEND OF THE LEMON BUBBLE

The second Penn spotted the Forest of Candy in the distance, his grumpy mood seemed to melt away. He instantly forgot about his fight with Kristy. And that her head was invisible.

Penn was excited to focus on what was in front of them—lots and lots of candy. Just as Lillibop had described, the landscape was littered with patches of different types of sweets: Chili Candy Canes that grew out of the ground, rolling hillocks covered with Sour Squishers, and hundreds of Fudgy Finches perched on the tree branches (which, according to the guide, were made of chocolate bark).

"I can't believe this is real!" Penn shook his head.

"Neither can I!" he heard her say.

The kids took off through the rows of Chili Candy Canes and across the Glittering Gumdrop field, laughing as they scooped up handfuls of the jellied treats. Penn recognized them from Turdgon's candy guide, so he knew that they were safe to eat. He popped them into his mouth and the sugar crystals literally danced on his tongue. Penn wasn't sure how, but they even *tasted* like colors. He shoved more of them into his pockets for later.

He stopped and turned to Kristy, feeling guilty. "Can you eat any of this?"

"Just because you can't see my mouth doesn't mean I don't still have it. And my mouth can still eat candy."

Penn could imagine her determined expression. She was being shockingly calm about the whole invisible-head thing. Girls were so weird.

"What are these ones?" Kristy called, holding up two swirly pink puffs.

Penn scanned his guide. "Those are Cinnamon Clouds."

"They're so fluffy!" Kristy yelled, shoving them into where her mouth probably was.

"I didn't finish! It says, 'Warning, you may sneeze jellybeans.'"

Kristy sneezed and sure enough, pretty little jellybeans shot out everywhere. "Ow." She rubbed what he assumed was her nose. "And ew." The baby dragons chomped them up off the ground.

Penn pulled some little purple pellets from a bird's nest. "These are Cuckoo-Nuts. It says they make you talk fast." They each ate just one of the chewy little nubs.

"I'm-not-talking-fast-are-you-talking-fast?"

"I-can't-hear-you-you're-talking-too-fast."

"I-have-so-many-business-ideas!-Look-how-high-I-can-jump."

"Abcdefghijklmnopqrstuvwxyz-Okay-thank-you-goodbye."

Then they both barfed a little and took a five-second nap.

The baby dragons watched in fascination as Kristy and Penn helped themselves to every kind of candy they could find, stuffing their satchels till they looked like they might pop at the seams.

Of course, they remembered their promises to grab Sour Squishers for Lillibop and Fudgy Finches for Turdgon. But there was only one type of candy that Penn truly cared about.

"Penn, over here!" Kristy shouted through an invisible mouthful of chewed-up chocolate bark. "I found the Lemon Bubbles!" Penn dropped his fistfuls of Sherbet Stars and raced over. At long last, the object of his quest was floating right in front of him. They looked just like he'd imagined—yellow and iridescent. Each time one popped, it would leave a fresh citrus scent in the air.

He froze. Why was he frozen?

This was what he wanted. This was everything these last couple of crazy days had been about.

"Penn? Are you okay?" Kristy asked.

He nodded. How could he admit to her that he was scared? Grabagorns didn't get scared, and if they did, they certainly didn't admit it. But what would happen after he ate the Lemon Bubble? He could never go back home. Would he have to be like Lillibop and find a sideways tugboat in a tree somewhere and live alone forever?

"Penn?" Kristy put her hand on his shoulder. He wasn't used to someone being that close to him who wasn't trying to punch him. It felt nice. "It's okay if you're scared."

It was like Kristy was a mind reader sometimes.

"What if . . . what if it doesn't work? What if there's too much monster in me? But also, what if it does work? Then . . . what am I? Who am I? Where do I belong?"

"Penn, you're going to be okay. Just remember that the good inside you is stronger than the bad. And that no matter what happens after you eat that Lemon Bubble, you're still you."

He wiped at his eye. Some sugar must have blown into it or something. "Okay, here goes..." Penn reached his blue paw out and let a bubble land gently in his palm. He lifted it to his mouth and took a bite. Penn squeezed his eyes shut as the bubble burst inside his mouth. It tasted sweet, citrusy, and...really familiar, actually.

"Did it work?" Penn asked, opening his eyes. He looked down at his hands, hopeful. But they were still all blue and monstery. His heart sank a little.

"Maybe it takes a few minutes to kick in," offered Kristy. She sounded like she was trying to convince herself. It didn't give Penn much confidence.

"Or maybe it wasn't enough?" Penn chomped down on three more bubbles. Why did he know this taste? He was positive he'd never had a Lemon Bubble before. Penn stared at his hands, waiting for something to happen... but nothing did. "Why isn't it working?"

All this way for a stupid Lemon Bubble and it didn't even do anything? The monster inside Penn began to rattle its cage. "This isn't FAIR!" Penn raged. He jumped up and down in frustration, squashing the Coconut Grass under his massive feet. Suddenly, he felt strange. Something had definitely changed.

"My other foot!" Penn cried out, kicking it into the air. Now *both* of his feet looked just like Brandon's—ugly, hairy, and blue. They ached in his now too-small, split-open shoes, so he tore the shoes off.

Somehow, the Lemon Bubble was having the opposite effect on him. He was becoming even more Grabagorny than before! Penn had worried at the beginning that it had been a lie—a story used to lure him into helping the women.

And he was right. He hated that he was right. The nerve of those wicked Rainbow Knights! They went on and on about helping people, but all they did was trick him for their own gain.

"She lied thooo me, Krithty!" Penn wailed as his lips began to change color. "Lermon thubbles don't help—"

The sound of laughter rumbled through the trees. And the smell of raccoon breath.

Penn knew that laugh. He'd heard it a thousand times before.

"Look at you, Penn. You're nearly one of us," Grabagorn Prime bellowed as he stepped out of his golf cart, flanked by his two bumbling henchmen—Grabagul and Grabaleg—and a dozen other Grabagorns. Landon, Brandon, and another Grabagorn who looked familiar stood behind them.

"Marcus!" Penn cried, realizing that his friend had fully transformated.

"His name is Grabagus now," Grabagorn Prime said. "And soon you'll join him. How do you like the sound of 'Grabaprisoner'?"

Penn did not like the sound of it at all. He pawed at his face to see if there were any normal parts of himself left. He turned to Kristy, feeling hopeless. He wished he could see her face. "I thourght the Lermon Brubbles would thurn eee barck!"

Before Kristy could respond, Grabagorn Prime stepped in front of her.

"Well, actually, it's the opposite." Grabagorn Prime laughed. "It speeds up the process." He laughed more and harder. "We've been sprinkling it into the well water for years!"

So *that's* why it tasted so familiar! Penn and the other boys drank from the well after Garate practice every single day. The whole brotherhood had been consuming Lemon Bubbles all along, without even realizing it.

Penn fell to his knees, crushed by this new information. Had everyone been lying to him about everything since forever?

"Don't feel bad, boy," Grabagorn Prime said, slapping Penn on the back. "There's no stopping it now. And once you fully transformate, you can never go back!" He had a huge smile on his face and was clearly enjoying watching Penn's world crumble.

Grabagorn Prime stuck out his pointy claw and popped a Lemon Bubble as it floated past his face. "It was very clever of me to spread the rumor that Lemon Bubbles stopped the process! I knew becoming the publisher of *Candy Every-Other-Monthly* would pay off someday."

"Yeah, man," Grabaleg said. "That was dope!"

"It was also the easiest way to catch traitors…like you." He pointed right at Penn. "You know what we call traitors now?"

"Free to go?" tried Penn.

"Penn!" Grabagorn Prime said. "We call them Penns! Now seize them! Throw them all in the dungeon pit!"

As soon as Grabagorn Prime gave the signal, ten more angry Grabagorns appeared, surrounding Penn, Kristy, and the baby dragons. The Grabagorns poked their spears at the baby dragons' backs.

There was nowhere left to run. Penn felt helpless.

He finally understood what it was like to be the prey caught in one of his traps.

12

THE LEGEND OF THE GREAT SCORCH

They didn't come all this way to be dragged back to North Greemulax. A familiar vibration in the sky caught Kristy's attention, and she knew she just had to stall until it came closer.

Kristy looked around at all the angry Grabagorns and refused to let them scare her. "Stop that!" she yelled at the ones poking the dragons. Which made them turn their spears on her. "Don't you dare come near me!"

"She's pretty dang feisty for a headless girl," Grabagorn Prime said. "Isn't she, boy?" He knocked Penn on the shoulder. "Tell her to behave."

"*She* has a name," Penn said. "And a head. It's just invisible right now."

Penn's attempt to stick up for her made Kristy smile.

"Penn?" she said.

"Kristy?" he replied.

"Get ready."

"Huh?"

Suddenly the vibration became a loud hum, and as all the Grabagorns looked up, Kristy grabbed one of the spears pointed at her and pulled Penn toward her. Together they pushed the baby dragons out of harm's way just as Trolley 4 burst through the clouds.

Jackelion's husky voice echoed through the loudspeakers: "Step away from the kids! I repeat, leave Penn and Kristy alone."

The Grabagorns didn't even wait for Grabagorn Prime's instructions. They just scrambled like big, blue babies, tripping over one another in a desperate attempt to hide from the mysterious flying vehicle.

"That's right!" X shouted from the trolley window. "Run, you cowards! We're Rainbow Knights and we're not afraid!" X was so bright that she reflected a million tiny rainbows onto the candyscape below.

One of the baby dragons tried to eat the rainbows off the ground, but Kristy pulled him back to safety. "We don't have time for that incredible cuteness, Buster. Also, I hope you don't mind, but in my head I've named you Buster."

Jackelion bellowed through the speaker

again. "Grabagorns, your actions have left us no choice but to activate the Turd gun."

"It's pronounced Tur-*jon*." Turdgon popped his head out and waved proudly. "My parents were French Canadian clowns."

"Once Turdgon commences wailing, you will have ten seconds. If Turdgon reaches his highest pitch, your Grabagorn heads will explode."

"*Aaahhh aaahhh ahhhhh, whoaaah aaah aaaah aaah*," Turdgon sang. It was the loudest, highest sound Kristy had ever heard. But it just kept getting louder and higher.

Grabaleg and Grabagul couldn't handle it. They took off, abandoning their posts by Grabagorn Prime's side.

"What are you losers doing?!" Grabagorn Prime barked into the chaos. "Come back here!"

Turdgon took a giant breath to deliver his final brain-busting note, when suddenly—

"*SCREEEEEEEE!*"

"What the foop? That wasn't me."

Just then, a massive green dragon soared over the landscape of candy, shooting blasts of fire at the ground. Grabagorns jumped out of the way, and Kristy and Penn did the same.

Two more adult dragons were fast approaching. They joined in the screeching and fire-blasting as they swooped down. In the middle of the madness, Jackelion landed the trolley safely on the marsh of Marshmallow Balloons.

As soon as they touched down, Jackelion and X jumped out and ran to Kristy.

"Kristy! Your head is gone! What did you do?" Jackelion scolded.

"Don't head-shame her," X said.

Kristy knew there was no time to explain now. Or to worry if she would ever look complete again. The three ladies took their Rainbow Knight defense stances. Their armor shone in the sunlight.

Meanwhile, the big green dragon landed near one of the babies. The other two dragons landed beside her.

"*Ror*...uh...I can't remember the word for *friends*?" Kristy said to the green one.

The babies began jumping up and down, flapping their wings excitedly. They started conversing in rapid Dragonese, explaining each part of their journey in great detail. Kristy was only able to follow part of it, but eventually the parents' expressions changed.

"Thank you," the green one said in perfect Human. She bowed her head to Kristy and Penn. "We appreciate all that you did. You are the enemy of our enemy, which makes you our new best friends."

"I don't believe in enemies, but I love new best friends!" Kristy said, grateful that they spoke her language and they weren't freaking out about her missing head. "Maybe you can help us? See, the Grabagorns are trying to kidnap us and imprison us in North Greemulax. Which I know happened to you once, too."

"They weren't imprisoned!" Landon cried out. "They attacked our land!"

"That was a lie," Penn said. "They didn't attack us. The dragons only burned down our land when they were helping their friends escape."

"That's a lie!" Brandon said. He turned to Grabagorn Prime. "Right?"

Grabagorn Prime shrugged. "Oh gorn up, it was just cave talk. If protecting my brotherhood is a lie, then call me a handsome, smart liar."

Penn turned to the dragons. "He told us you killed all the women, too."

"You pinned everything on us?" the green dragon yelled. "That is so wack!"

"It was not *wack*. We wanted them to blame you instead of us! We wanted them to transformate! And it worked!"

"Pretty rotten, right?" Kristy replied.

"Who cares?" Grabagorn Prime snarled. "Have you kids forgotten who you are? You're people! *Dragons* are the enemy!" He pointed to a smoldering hole in the ground beside him. "Witness their destruction for yourselves."

Kristy saw her chance. Maybe the Power of One could help. Even though he was literally the worst, Grabagorn Prime was a One, too. Maybe if she could change his mind, it would put an end to all of this.

Kristy stepped forward. "Mr. Prime, none of us have to be enemies! Have you ever thought about that?"

"And maybe no one has to scorch anyone . . ." Penn added. "Or be trapped in a prison pit?"

"Yeah! We could all be friends." Kristy was feeling pretty bold. She continued. "Best friends! And no one would have to fight again. We could all just look out for each other instead!"

Grabagorn Prime walked slowly toward Kristy and leaned down. "And how do you, little girl, suggest that we do that?"

"Well . . ." Kristy thought for a moment.

"Kristy, your mouth is back!" Penn said.

"Ugh," Grabagorn Prime said. "The worst part."

Kristy ignored him and continued. "I think the first thing to do would be for you to apologize to the dragons. Then the women. And to all the boys you lied to. We could all talk about what went wrong before and—"

Grabagorn Prime let out a thunderous cackle.

"That's the problem with you women! All

you do is talk, talk, TALK!" Grabagorn Prime stomped his gigantic feet and narrowed his bulgy eyes. "No. There will be NO TALKING! We must fight!" At this, Grabagorn Prime twisted himself into his most intimidating Garate pose. "Let's do this."

Kristy gulped. Okay, so maybe best friends was a reach.

13

THE LEGEND OF THE CANDY CANE

Grabagorn Prime began to punch at the air around him. Penn noticed for the first time that Garate moves didn't actually look super effective, especially against a dragon whose head was ten feet in the air.

The three adult dragons surrounded Grabagorn Prime. The green dragon shot a fire blast at his left foot. The hairs on top caught fire, and Grabagorn Prime whimpered as he tried to put them out.

The dragons laughed.

The dragons were speaking among themselves, possibly discussing how best to defeat Grabagorn Prime, when *another* magic trolley burst through the clouds. It floated to the ground, gentle as a feather. It was in much better shape than Trolley 4.

Everyone held their breath as two powerful women stepped out. The Grabagorns gawked. They were not used to seeing women. One of the women wore a glittering golden crown. The other wore a lot of chunky jewelry.

"Lillibop!" Penn smiled, running over to her. Seeing her again made him feel safe and calm. "What are you doing here?"

"I decided...that I couldn't risk losing you again."

Penn didn't understand. She hadn't lost him before. Had she? The recurring dream of Pudding Lake came rushing back to him. A detail he had previously missed now seemed clear as day: In his dream, he clung to the back of a woman with golden spaghetti hair and chunky jewelry.

Lillibop nodded, her big eyes brimming with tears. "When you walked into my tugboat, I...I couldn't believe it was really you."

Penn couldn't believe he was about to say this word, but it just came out. *"Mom?"*

"Whoa," said Kristy.

"No! Sweetheart, look at me. I'm sixty-five." She shook her head at Grabagorn Prime. "Don't you do any kind of Reproductive Health class with these boys?"

"We have double PE," snapped the monster.

Lillibop took Penn's face in her hands. "Penn, I'm your grandma. And I love you very much."

"Double whoa," Kristy said.

"If you're my grandma, where's my . . ." Penn didn't finish his question because he realized the answer.

Lillibop hung her head. "Your mom didn't make it across the lake that day. But she's the reason so many of us did. Your mom died a hero. And all this time I thought I lost you, too. I didn't want to say anything in case it would upset you and cause you to transformate faster!"

"But you tried to save me! I remember!" Now Penn's eyes were starting to well up with tears, too. And he didn't even try to hide it. "I dreamed about it!" He reached his big, blue arms around her and pulled her toward him. He was getting much better at these hug things.

"My little monster . . ." Lillibop touched Penn's face. "As soon as you left my tugboat, I knew I had to follow you. I pressed the rainbow button on my wall. It's a direct line to

Queen Lorianna," she explained. "She eventually came to pick me up in her trolley."

"So *that's* what the rainbow button is for," Kristy said. "I thought it released a rainbow slide! This is good, too, though."

"Kristy!" Lillibop said when she realized it was her. "What did I tell you about staying solid?"

As Lillibop lectured Kristy, Queen Lorianna the Wobbly approached Grabagorn Prime.

"Come on, Gregg," she said, shaking her head. "Don't you think it's finally time to rethink this whole monster thing? It's not really working out for anyone in Greemulax."

"Greg?" Penn laughed.

"Gregg," Lorianna said with a smile. "With two *g*'s at the end."

"*G* is the best letter," Grabagorn Prime said.

"How did we come from the same parents?" said Queen Lorianna.

Same parents? They were sister and brother?

Lorianna sighed and turned to Graba—*Gregg.* "So what do you say, brother? Can we put this whole thing behind us and start anew? As one Greemulax?"

The Rainbow Knights and Grabagorns held their breath as they waited to hear their respective leaders' decision. Lorianna raised her eyebrows at her brother.

Lillibop whispered to the children, "He'll never go for it."

"Why not?" pleaded Penn.

Lillibop sighed. " 'Cause when you have *all* the marbles for a long time, and then someone says you gotta *share* 'em—it feels like you're losing your marbles."

The children nodded, but they didn't really get it.

"Never!" Grabagorn Prime growled.

"Okay then, Gregg." Queen Lorianna shook

her head. "Have it your way. We'll battle!" She walked over to a row of Chili Candy Canes sticking out of the ground and yanked one out. The queen closed her eyes. Power began to swirl around her hand and onto the candy, transforming it into a fiery sword!

"Ooooooh," said the Grabagorns.

"Ahhhhhh," said the Rainbow Knights.

"Girl's on fire!" yelled Turdgon. "Werk, Actual Kween!"

"Okay, knights, get in formation," Lorianna ordered. The Rainbow Knights followed suit, plucking Chili Candy Canes from the ground. Penn watched as Kristy's burst into flames in her hand. He wanted one of those, too. Plus, whoa, he could see Kristy's hair now. It was as fiery red as the sword.

"Penn! Catch!" Kristy called out as she tossed him a fiery sword. But as soon as it touched his Grabagorny hands, it fell to the ground, hitting his foot on the way.

"Ouch!" Penn's heart sank. "I can't hold it with these paws!"

X ran forward to spar with Grabagul. She thrust her fire sword in front of her, and the giant monster jumped out of the way. "That's right. You leave us alone!"

While everyone was distracted, Penn saw his chance. Maybe he could stop this fight another way—with the truth. He found Landon and Brandon hiding under a pile of fur pelts, stress-eating Chewy Chums.

"I've mithed you guyth!" Penn exclaimed. He took a deep breath and spoke slowly so they could understand him through his confusing lisp. "I mean...I've *missed* you guys. I keep thinking about all of our days spent hanging out in our favorite pit together. All those food fights at Night Meal. Remember the time Marcus threw a piece of roasted meat at Grabaleg's back hair and it stuck there? No one even noticed for hours!" Penn laughed and shook his head.

"You deserted us!" Landon said.

"Yeah, don't think we've forgotten what a total Penn you are," Brandon added.

"Still hurtful," Penn said. "But can we please go back to being friends?"

"No, you're a traitor," Landon huffed. "Grabagorn Prime said that—"

"He's been lying to us about everything!" Penn said. "Not only about the dragons. He lied about our mothers and he lied about who we are inside! Grabagorn Prime just wants to keep us all monsters because *he* is a monster. The question is: Do you want to be monsters?"

Brandon and Landon looked at each other.

Penn knew what they were thinking, because he had thought the same thing. For almost as long as they could remember, every day had been spent the same way. Everything they did—from participating in the SuperCup to practicing their daily Garate—had been in pursuit of a goal. To become Grabagorns. It was easier to let someone else make the decisions. It was easier to go with the flow. But what did they want to be? Who were they really?

"Actually, no," Brandon finally admitted. "I kind of want to be a dragon vet. I have always secretly thought dragons were cool. And now that I know they didn't cause the Great Scorch, I like them even more!"

"I want to play guitar!" The words burst forth from Landon's lips as if they'd been sitting on the edge of them for years.

The two boys stood up tall, ready to join Penn in battle. They took their Garate stances, but this time they faced Grabagorn Prime.

"You boys are weak and useless!" he bellowed. "I have to do everything MYSELF, don't I?" Then the giant Grabagorn started stuffing his face with as many Lemon Bubbles as he could reach. Yellow drool dripped from his hairy chin, and his expression turned even more wild.

What was he doing? Penn wondered.

Grabagorn Prime started to grow. His body became larger and larger as he cackled with delight. In just a few moments, he had grown so big that he towered over every Grabagorn, Rainbow Knight, and dragon.

"Run, Lillibop," Lillibop yelled.

"I will crush you all!" Grabagorn Prime roared.

This time, everyone believed him.

THE LEGEND OF UNMONSTERING

The Rainbow Knights and Grabagorns scattered across the Forest of Candy like a jellybean sneeze. They darted behind marshmallows and gummies, narrowly dodging being squished under Grabagorn Prime's giant feet. Kristy, Jackelion, and X thrashed their fire swords at the hanging Sugar Vines that blocked a candy cave. They had finally gotten inside when Kristy saw Penn trip and fall face-first into a Chocolate Mud puddle.

"I've got you, Penn!" She raced back out from her hiding place, took him by the paw, and pulled him out of the sludge. Once he was freed, the two of them grabbed Landon and Brandon. The twins stood frozen with shock, watching as their gigantic leader thrashed and roared with ugly rage. It was a lot to take in.

"This way, boys." Kristy spread her arms wide to protect them as she ushered them to a safety huddle inside the cave. "That's it . . . that's it. Everyone stay calm."

"Dude! One of your eyebrows came back!" Landon said.

"Which one?" Kristy asked. "Penelope or Oona?"

"How would I know the answer to that?"

The dragons weren't afraid. They stood

their ground, flapping their impressive wings and blasting Grabagorn Prime's legs with fire. But it had little effect on the beast. He just laughed. Then he bent down, picked the dragons up by their tails, and tossed them all the way to East Greemulax.

"Even the dragons couldn't beat him?!" Landon shouted in disbelief. "What are we gonna do?!"

Kristy racked her brain for ideas. She hadn't been a Rainbow Knight for very long, but this was definitely the most intense situation that she'd encountered. By the looks on Jackelion's and X's faces, they felt the same. "What *are* we gonna do?"

Penn stood, solemn. He spoke slowly so he could pronounce the words clearly through his monster lips. "I know what needs to be done." He took a deep breath, like he was trying to summon the strength to even say the words out loud. "Only a monster can beat another monster. Landon, Brandon, and I must give in to our anger and transformate. Then we can grow big and, well . . . show him the Roundpit."

Kristy shook his shoulder. "Penn, no! Once you become a Grabagorn, you can never change back. There has to be another way!"

"Like my mother before me, I'm ready to sacrifice myself for the greater good."

Jackelion and X leaned on the handles of their fire swords for support.

"Maybe let him be a monster. We need backup *now*," X wheezed. "It's dozens against just us."

"No!" Kristy shouted. She wished the boys had another way to fight alongside them. She wished they could use the swords. But a lot would have to change for that to happen. Then Kristy remembered what Lillibop had told her back in the tree house tugboat. No one could shine on the outside if they didn't feel it on the inside. Change had to come from within.

Kristy had an idea. A great idea. "Boys, listen to me!"

But the twins were busy arguing about who got to sit on which candy rock. They didn't even notice Kristy was trying to get their attention.

"Guys, lirsen to Krrrrrrithy!" Penn yelled at the top of his lungs. As soon as he said the words, his lips began to turn back to the normal pink color that they had originally been. Could it be true?

"Your lips!" Kristy pointed. "They're . . . *unmonstering*!"

"What? How?!" Penn touched his mouth. He smiled.

"I know how." Kristy took Penn by his shoulders. "Remember when you let me read the map?"

"And my ear stopped buzzing!"

Penn and Kristy were now completely in sync. "By listening and supporting others, men can unmonster!"

Landon wrinkled his nose. "That doesn't sound that fun."

"Neither does wiping your butt, but you learned how to do it!" Kristy blurted. Then all the females froze in grossified fear. "You did learn how do to that, right?"

The boys all chimed in. "Yes." "Of course." "We're not *total* monsters."

"Hey, your head is back," Brandon noted.

Perfect timing, Kristy thought. She raised her fire sword into the air triumphantly. "And once you unmonster, you can use our fire swords!"

Brandon jumped to his feet. "I like your idea. Let's try it." As soon as he said it, his eyebrows and nose shrank back down to human size. "Whoa. How else can we work together?"

"Well, we need more fire swords!" Kristy

bit her lip. She scanned the top of the cave and spotted a small grouping of Chili Candy Canes poking down from the ceiling. But they were really high up. "Human pyramid! Brandon, you and Jackelion are the biggest. You form a base."

"How dare you," Jackelion complained as she took her place.

"Landon and X, you stand on their backs and lift me up." Kristy stepped up and into their grip. As they hoisted her up, Landon's ugly monster paws changed back into strong human hands.

"It's working!" he cried.

But the candies were still out of reach.

"Okay, Penn, you climb up our backs!"

Penn was nervous. That was pretty high up.

"Don't worry, dude, we got you," said Brandon, causing his feet and neck to unmonster.

Penn climbed up onto Jackelion and Brandon, over Landon and X, up next to Kristy, and then, balancing himself against the wall of the cave, onto her shoulders. Penn reached his blue paw up toward the Chili Candy Canes, but they were still *just* out of reach. Frustration coursed through his body. "Arrrghhhh!" he growled and banged on the wall of the cave, sending the whole human pyramid teetering. Everyone shrieked in fear.

Once they regained their balance, Kristy spoke to him in a calm voice. "Penn, it's okay to be mad. Everyone gets mad. But use your words, not your fists, or we're all gonna break our necks."

"I'm mad that I can't reach it. And . . . I'm jealous that everyone else has unmonstered except me. And . . . and . . . I miss my mom."

"I'm sorry, buddy," said Landon.

"We miss our mom, too," said Brandon, now fully back to the black-haired boy he used to be. Penn felt sweaty and a little light-headed. But in a good way, like after a long race.

He felt the cool wetness of the cave walls as his paws unmonstered and turned into hands. His shoulders unmonstered. And he could stretch more. He took a deep breath and reached the last few inches . . . and he got them! The cluster of Chili Candy Canes fell down into his arms. The magic could begin.

Once each boy had a fire sword in his freshly unmonstered hands, they were ready to go. The gang ran back out into the chaos, but this time they were united as a team. Too bad it was a total mess. In the time they'd been in the cave, the Forest of Candy had been almost demolished. There were pieces of broken, scorched candy everywhere. The entire place looked like a melted rainbow and smelled like toasted marshmallow.

Grabagorn Prime was sitting in the center of

the Hot Fudge Bog, breathing heavily. Apparently, growing massively was exhausting. Kristy saw it as the perfect opportunity to trick him.

"Do you still have that fishing net, Penn?" Kristy asked, poking his satchel. "The one Lillibop gave you?"

"Of course." Penn shrugged. "It's the most important part of any trap."

"Good." The boys listened as Kristy explained her idea: They would all sneak up on Grabagorn Prime—from different directions but at the same time. Then they would poke him with their fire swords to distract him. While Grabagorn Prime was dealing with his tiny burns, Kristy and Penn would throw the net over him and secure him down.

"Okay, on three..." Kristy called out to the troops. "One...two..." Everyone held their fire swords at the ready. "THREE!"

The Rainbow Knights charged, whooping

and hollering "Pancakes for dinner!" (which was also their battle cry) as they jabbed Grabagorn Prime with their flaming weapons. The boys joined in, following the girls' lead this time.

"Ouch!" Grabagorn Prime wailed. "That stings! Stop it!" He swatted them away but was far too slow. The net was already over him. Kristy was surprised at how easy it was to hold the giant beast down. Maybe Grabagorn Prime wasn't so strong, after all.

"Well done!" Queen Lorianna cheered. She looked straight at Kristy and smirked. "Maybe Gregg will finally calm down now that he's been swaddled." Lorianna shook her head at Grabagorn Prime and sighed. "You big baby!"

The Rainbow Knights giggled and congratulated one another on the victory, but they kept their grip firmly on the net. There was no way they were going to risk letting him get away. They held their ground, standing tall and proud of themselves. Kristy felt energy coursing through her whole body and knew she was as solid as she'd ever been. She caught Penn's eye across the net, and they smiled at each other like kids in a candy forest.

Even though everyone was celebrating, there was still something wrong. The queen was pacing back and forth. She looked nervous. Penn and the Rainbow Knights watched as Lorianna took a small step toward Grabagus and his father, Grabagruff. She had tears in her eyes.

But Queen Lorianna didn't seem sad. She was hopeful. "Jonavan. Marcus. Don't you remember me at all? Won't you try and unmonster? For me?"

"*Mother?*" Marcus said, unsure. He searched his father's eyes for the truth.

Grabagruff nodded. It was true. Queen Lorianna the Wobbly was, indeed, his mother. They had been a family once upon a time.

"But it's too late for me!" Marcus cried, collapsing onto the ground. "I'm already all monster. I can't turn back."

"I don't think that's true anymore," said the queen, reaching her arms toward her son. "I have seen such a display of courage and growth in all of you. You are not the same as the Grabagorns we left behind. You boys—and girls—can choose to be whoever you want to be. Yes, it might be hard. It might take a little time. But it's possible . . . if it's important to you."

The boy and his father shared a knowing look. Of course they wanted to try. They'd spent far too long away from her as it was.

"You got this, guys!" Kristy cheered. She gave her section of the net over for X to hold and ran over to the queen's men. Kristy knew she could help put them back together again. She held up both her hands and gave them the biggest smile. "High five if you want to turn back?"

Marcus and Jonavan hesitated. As they left her hanging, Kristy felt someone walk up and stand by her side. It was Penn.

"You can do it, Marcus," Penn said.

Suddenly, they brought their hands up to meet Kristy's. Then the father and son looked at each other and high-fived. Kristy's heart swelled as she watched Marcus and Jonavan walk toward the queen. With each step the two took, their feet began to change. They were becoming men again!

Penn and the twins sprang into action. They went around and showed the rest of the Grabagorns ways that they could try to unmonster, too. The sound of high fives echoed like applause. Everyone was becoming one team again.

Kristy was amazed at the transformations.

Each time a Grabagorn changed back, it was like he was remembering who he was. The men smiled and laughed and even hugged. But somehow they all still had random blue tufts of hair on their bodies. "What's up with the blue hair?" Kristy asked.

"Ah, yes." The queen nodded knowingly. "That's because the monster is always inside. We don't have to destroy it.... We just have to learn to tame it. Are you all willing to learn to do that?"

The men agreed—they would love to learn something new. Taming their inner monster seemed like the perfect place to start. But there was one Grabagorn who didn't like the idea.

"Not me! Not ever!" Grabagorn Prime wrestled with his net. "In fact, I want to become even *more* of a monster!"

"Well, there's only one way to do that." Lillibop held out a Red Sugar Dot. "This candy will turn you into a monster forever. If you eat this, there's no going back."

"GIVE IT TO ME!" Grabagorn Prime reached his claw through the net and snatched it out of Lillibop's palm. He tossed it into his mouth. A moment passed, but nothing happened. "Did it work? Am I a monster forever?" As he talked, his voice got higher and his body began to shrink. "Why is that rock getting bigger? Wait a minute, why do I feel so cute all of a sudden?" He became smaller and smaller, until he was the size of a little Grabagorn doll.

"Oh, it worked." Lillibop scooped him up into her hands and smirked.

"You lied to me!"

"If protecting all of Greemulax makes her a liar," Kristy said, "then call her a gorgeous golden-spaghetti-haired liar."

"Ooooh." Turdgon skipped over and poked

the teensy Grabagorn. His angry barks now sounded high-pitched and cute. "Look, a pet!" Lillibop passed the little monster over to Turdgon, who tied a tiny bow in his blue fur.

"Grandma, do women ever have blue fur?" Penn asked.

"Ugh, sweetheart, are you kidding me? You should see my armpits!"

They all laughed.

When the queen announced that it was time to go home, nobody argued. They had a lot of rebuilding to do. "Kristy? Penn? Would you two do me the honor of riding home in my trolley?" Lorianna smiled. "You too, Lillibop. Come ride with your grandson."

Everyone piled in and sat down. Penn sat between his best friend, Kristy, and his grandmother. "Trolley!" the queen ordered. "Go home! To *Northwest* Greemulax."

"Got it. Purchasing 'For Best CHEESY SNAX'!" the trolley chirped and took off into the brilliant sunset.

Some things never change, thought Kristy. But a lot of stuff can.

15

THE LEGEND OF GOOD
AND BAD

As the sunlight streamed in through the open window and warmed his face, Penn thought about how lucky he felt. In NoWeGreem (the new Northwest Greemulax), there was no Garate practice, which left time for school. But real school, with teachers and textbooks, instead of Grabacoach and cave drawings.

Penn was learning all sorts of new, fascinating things.

Today, Penn sat cross-legged on a purple velvet pillow with his eyes closed. He concentrated on Turdgon's soothing voice. "And another deep breath in through your nose... and exhale through your mouth... and when you're ready, open your eyes."

Penn blinked himself back to the room and was greeted by the warm, happy faces of his friends: Kristy, Marcus, Landon, Brandon, and a new friend called Maria. She was good at math and had the best laugh. Everyone laughed a lot more now that they were all together.

"Today's topic, children, is something called mindfulness," Turdgon explained. He put a flourish on the end of each sentence. Now that he was a teacher, Turdgon felt like he was giving an important performance every single day. "That means you take the time to notice the moment you are in and to enjoy it."

Penn didn't think he'd have a hard time with this one. Ever since the Grand Unmonstering, he had spent every day feeling pretty good.

Turdgon flipped his scarf over his shoulder. "Also, mindfulness can mean that we all think about our actions and stuff, you know? Why don't we go around and say how we are going to practice mindfulness. Kristy, go ahead."

"Thanks, Turgs!" Kristy smiled. Her sunny demeanor had become even brighter these days. "I vow to be mindful by always speaking my truth! Like, if I understand how I feel— even if I'm angry—it totally helps to tell someone instead of burying my feelings. Then I can stay solid and bright—and keep my head— all the time!" Her eyes glittered.

"Very good, very good." Turdgon nodded.

Penn went next. "Every day, I am mindful that I have the power to tame the monster inside me! I just have to be aware of my inner Grabagorn and not let him take over."

Turdgon was pleased enough with this. "Good, children, yes, yes..." he said, walking over to the corner of the room. A small stage with red velvet curtains had been set up. "Now that we've talked about *that*, I think it's time for some theater! Who wants a part in my new play, *Pudding on the Ritz! A Musical* by Turdgon A. Puddingman?"

Obviously, everyone did.

A commotion outside caught their attention, and the students all rushed to the window. Penn saw Gregg being chased by one of Lillibop's cats.

"Okay, children, the Gregg and cat show is over. Time for my show! Penn, could you

bring that heavy chest of costumes over here?"
Turdgon squealed with delight. "Because I . . .
don't want to."

"No problem!" Penn replied. "I might
not have monster arms anymore, but I'm still
pretty strong." But as Penn bent down and
lifted the chest up, his arms turned blue.
Penn dropped the chest to the floor in a
panic. As soon as he did, his arms turned back
to normal.

"Oh, that," Turdgon said with a wave of
his hand. "That happens to me all the time.
It's the only way I can open my mayonnaise
jars. So it's not all bad! Just control the monster, and you'll be fine. Now bring the costumes over! I have a fringe shawl I want to try
on you."

"Do you want some help, Penn?" Kristy
offered. She knew now that strength and
support went both ways. It wasn't just a

boys-supporting-girls thing. It was an every-one-supporting-one-another thing. She also knew that she had both good and bad inside her, too. And every day was a new chance to choose to do good.

AWESOME DRAWING BY THE AUTHOR.

BLACK-AND-WHITE SO YOU CAN COLOR IT IN!

ACKNOWLEDGMENTS

I could not have for realsies written this without the help of Sarah Mlynowski and Gillian Berrow. Thanks to Farrin Jacobs, Sam Means, Meredith Scardino, and Pam Gruber for all the notes you slipped into my backpack. And even though I loved my original cover and art, I'm grateful to Brandon Dorman for making my characters come to life—without ever tracing!

Special thanks to my agent, Jacqueline White. She wasn't a huge supporter until someone else was interested, but she figured out the contracts, so contractually I have to thank her. Also a big "shout-out" to all my exclamation points!!!!! I could not have done this without you, guys!!!!!

I also couldn't have done it without these nice people from my publisher and beyond: Reagan Arthur, Emily Ashcraft, Rick Ball, Danielle Cantarella, Jackie Engel, Jen Graham, Karina Granda, Sasha Illingworth, Hannah Milton, Marisa Finkelstein, Samantha Shanker, Erin Slonaker, Megan Tingley, and Ruiko Tokunaga. High fives to you all.

And of course thanks to Titus, Lillian, Cyndee, Gretchen, and Donna Maria, for always helping me take it ten seconds at a time.

Eric Leibowitz/Netflix/Universal Television

Kimberly Cougar Schmidt was born on a roller coaster during a tornado alert. She was the top-rated babysitter in Durnsville, Indiana, from 1997 until March 1998, when some stuff happened. In 2015 she appeared on the *Today Show*! Kimmy got her GED and went on to not graduate with a degree in philosophy from Columbia University (not to be confused with Columbia House, which is big enough to bring you all the best in entertainment). When not enjoying candy for dinner, Kimmy can be found smiling and going outside. She is also working on engineering a device that would make it possible for humans to high-five squirrels. She lives in New York City with her friends and her pet horse, Horse-o the Giant Dog. This is her first book! She is not garbage.